W9-BOA-733

CHANCES ARE

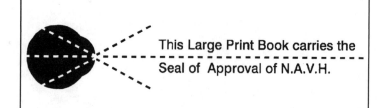

This Large Print Book carries the Seal of Approval of N.A.V.H.

CHANCES ARE

DONNA HILL

THORNDIKE PRESS

A part of Gale, Cengage Learning

GALE
CENGAGE Learning™

Detroit • New York • San Francisco • New Haven, Conn • Waterville, Maine • London

GALE
CENGAGE Learning

Thorndike Press® Large Print African-American.
The text of this Large Print edition is unabridged.
Other aspects of the book may vary from the original edition.
Set in 16 pt. Plantin.
Printed on permanent paper.

LIBRARY OF CONGRESS CATALOGING-IN-PUBLICATION DATA

Hill, Donna (Donna O.)
  Chances are / by Donna Hill.
    p. cm. — (Thorndike Press large print African-American)
  ISBN-13: 978-1-4104-1836-4 (hardcover : alk. paper)
  ISBN-10: 1-4104-1836-7 (hardcover : alk. paper)
  1. African American teenage mothers—Fiction. 2. African American television producers and directors—Fiction. 3. African Americans—Fiction. 4. Large type books. I. Title.
PS3558.I3864C47 2009
813'.54—dc22
                                    2009017428

Published in 2009 by arrangement with Harlequin Books S.A.

Printed in the United States of America
1 2 3 4 5 6 7 13 12 11 10 09

Chances Are is sincerely dedicated
to the wonderful young women
and their children who I had
the pleasure of working with in a setting
very much like Chances, and who
provided the inspiration for this
story. I think of you all often,
and wish you all
continued success and many blessings.

PROLOGUE

Fear, such as she'd never known, rose along her flesh like prickly heat then spread mercilessly through her slender seventeen-year-old frame. Every limb ached, partly from the uncontrollable tremors that rocked her, but mostly from the vicious beating inflicted upon her by her father — with the two-inch thick, black leather strap that he used to sharpen his razor — even as he prayed to God for forgiveness, and tears of remorse coursed down his tortured cheeks. If her mother hadn't finally pulled him off her, she was certain she'd be dead.

Cowering in the farthest corner of her bed, eyes swollen, throat raw from crying, she jumped at the sound of breaking glass and raised voices from the floor below. Her parents had been screaming and yelling at each other for what seemed an eternity. And it was all her fault. *Her fault.*

Oh, God, what would she give to turn

back the clock, use her head and remember all the lessons that had been drilled into her over the years? How could she ever face her mother again and not feel her shame, or face her father and not feel worthless and dirty? She didn't know if she ever could.

Fresh tears coursed down Dione's cheeks, surprising her. She was sure she'd had no more tears to shed. And then, suddenly, the three-story brownstone on Madison Street, grew silent, which was more frightening than the noise.

She sat up in the bed, listening. The front door slammed, rocking the house. Then she heard footsteps on the stairs. They were light. *Her mother.*

The door opened and her mother stepped into the dimness of the frilly, but precisely ordered bedroom. Margaret Williams didn't say a word, but went straight to Dione's closet, took out a suitcase and began pulling clothes off hangers then out of drawers, stuffing them inside.

Dione watched in silence, her horror mounting with each breath she took.

Her mother snapped the suitcase shut and turned toward her daughter, unable or unwilling to meet Dione's pleading eyes. She reached into the pocket of her pale peach robe, pulled out a thick, white enve-

8

lope and handed it to Dione.

"You have to leave. Now. Your father doesn't want you here when he gets back."

Dione's eyes widened in terror, her stomach lurched and seemed to rise to her chest. "Mommy, please! Don't let him do this to me."

"There's nothing I can do. I can't go against your father. I can't."

"Where can I go? What will I do?"

"You should have thought about that before —" Her voice broke. She turned away and walked toward the door.

"Ma, please! Please!" Dione scurried to the end of the bed and went after her mother, wrapping her arms around her mother's stiff body. "You can't let Daddy put me out," she begged as tears streamed down her face. "I have nowhere to go. I'll do anything. Hide me," she begged in desperation. "Please —"

She felt her mother's body tremble as she struggled to contain her sobs. "Don't be here when he gets back, Dione. For your own sake. I don't know if I can stop him if he goes after you again."

Dione dropped her arms to her sides, feeling as if the life had been sucked from her and she wished, at that moment, that her father had killed her, because it had to be

9

better than this.

"There's enough money in the envelope to last you awhile."

"And then what?" she choked. "What's going to happen to me when the money runs out? How can you let him do this to me? Do you even care?" she screamed at her mother's back.

Her mother took a breath and walked out, shutting the door and her daughter out of her life.

Through clouded, tear-filled eyes, Dione stared at the closed door and vowed from that night forward that no door would ever be closed to her again.

CHAPTER 1

Eighteen years later

Dione Williams sat in her small, but neat, afrocentric office, located on the basement level of the four-story brownstone she'd purchased five years earlier in the Clinton Hill section of Brooklyn. Laid out from end to end on the gray metal table she used for a desk — purchased at a discount city auction — were utility bills, invoices from vendors, taxes due and another pile of rejection letters for the three proposals she'd written for additional funding.

She rubbed a hand across her forehead, then began to massage her temples with the balls of her thumbs.

Chances Are was in trouble. Serious trouble, and according to her accountant if she didn't secure a solid influx of capital within the next four to six months, the ten teen mothers and their babies who'd come to live at the reconverted residence and who depended on her for their survival would be put out onto the street, and her staff would be out of jobs.

All around her, she felt the doors closing, and that old fear underscored by more than a decade of anger resurfaced like a swimmer gasping above the water for air. She looked up and out of the small basement window, catching a glimpse of the near-barren trees, the branches reaching out at her, begging for her help and the grass that was turning a honey brown before disappearing until next spring, were all symbolic of her life.

Sighing, Dione tucked a wayward strand of shoulder-length auburn hair behind her ear, her hand brushing against her damp cheek. There had to be a way to save her dream. Unfortunately, she'd completely run out of original ideas. And the one alternative was too far-fetched and much too risky. Absently she toyed with the tiny gold stud that adorned her lobe. There had to be another way.

The soft tap on the door momentartily drew her attention away from her disturbing thoughts. Quickly she wiped her tears away.

"Come in."

"Hey, Dione, I had a feeling I'd find you

12

down here." Brenda Frazier, her assistant director, right and left hand, breezed into the room and shut the door. "Do things really look as bad as the expression on your face?" She eased her hip along the edge of the desk.

Dione tried to smile. "I'm afraid so."

"What about the bank — can't we get a loan?"

"The building is mortgaged to the hilt. Without any substantial flow of capital, the bank won't front another loan."

Brenda folded her arms beneath her breasts. "Dee, we may have to go with the documentary thing. I mean if it works and we could get the attention we need and deserve —" Brenda's eyebrows rose.

Dione shook her head. "I can't do that to the girls, Brenda. Some of them are here because they've had to get out of abusive situations. There are others who don't want anyone to know where they are, or that they're homeless and living in a shelter."

Brenda threw her hands up in the air in frustration. "I wish I had such hard living. We may be *categorized* as a shelter, but these apartments are plenty fit for these queens. I wouldn't mind living in one of them myself. You've done miracles with this place and with these girls. People need to

13

know that."

Dione pressed her lips together. "Not at the expense of the girls' privacy, Bren."

If it was one thing that Dione was always adamant about, it was the privacy of the residents, Brenda knew. Dione guarded it as fiercely as a lioness governing her cubs. But even a lioness had to let her cubs out into the world. Dione couldn't protect the girls forever. "Why don't you put it to the girls for a vote? Have a house meeting. We all have a lot to lose if we have to close down. You more than anyone. You put your whole life into this place. And what about Niyah? Your salary pays for her education. And mine keeps a roof over my head. So, I don't know about you, but I'll be damned if I'm leaving without a fight."

Dione grinned. If there was one thing she could depend on Brenda for, it was a challenge. "All right." She blew out a breath. "Set up a house meeting for tomorrow night after dinner. And would you pull out the proposal for me? I want to take another look at it."

"Now you're talking." She patted Dione's hand. "It's going to work out, Dee. This may be just the opportunity we need."

"I hope so. For everyone's sake. What was that producer's name again?"

"Garrett Lawrence."

Slowly, Dione nodded. The last thing she needed was someone taping, and snooping into all of their business. But if it could save Chances Are, and the girls were willing, she'd have to take the risk. She'd just deal with the repercussions when they came, and she was certain they would. She only hoped that this Garrett Lawrence didn't have the sensitivity of a gnat.

Upstairs, the house, as usual, was full of activity for a Monday morning. The young mothers and their babies could be heard in their one-bedroom apartments dashing around in preparation for their day. On each of the four floors were three apartments, except on the ground floor where there were two. One of which was where Ms. Betsy lived, subbing as housemother during the night and childcare worker during the day. Each of the apartments was fully furnished with a small living room/dining room, bedroom, washer/dryer unit and full-sized bathroom. When Dione had purchased the house, she'd had it completely gutted and renovated to accommodate the number of rooms she needed. Although the original sprawling rooms had been cut down substantially, they still maintained a sense of warmth. She'd painstakingly selected every piece of furniture, every crib, bed, dinette set, sheet, towel, pot and pan. When the girls arrived they came into a place that they could immediately feel was home.

The girls were taught how to take care of their apartments, do laundry, shop on a budget, and cook and clean. All in preparation for them eventually leaving and moving out on their own. Dione's vision was to provide the girls with an environment that they wanted to aspire to. So many of them had come from places that only nightmares were made of. They hadn't been taught how to do anything, and even though they balked at the cooking classes, parenting and permanent housing workshops, she knew they appreciated it — appreciated the fact that someone had finally taken enough time to care about them and about their future.

Dione went up to the second floor and knocked on apartment 2B. Gina, their newest resident, was notorious for oversleeping, which always made her late for her GED classes at the local high school.

Ms. Betsy, "mother in spirit" to Dione, refused to coddle Gina by giving her a personal wake-up call every morning. It was Dione and Betsy's biggest bone of contention. So Dione had to sneak upstairs every morning and do it herself. There was no way she would sit back and let Gina sleep through opportunity. Maybe Gina did need some tough love, but Dione painfully remembered how desperately she'd needed love and nurturing and how she was turned out into the street. She couldn't let that happen to anyone else.

She pressed the bell that sat like a wad in the center of the heavy wood door and listened to the chime echo against the stillness inside, a sure sign that Gina was still asleep. Dione looked from side to side and peered over the railing while she waited, crossing her fingers and toes that Gina would get to the door before Ms. Betsy spotted her.

"Yes?" came a very groggy voice.

"Gina, it's me, Ms. Williams."

Gina cracked the door open, her micro-braided extensions that nearly reached her waist, shadowed her seventeen-year-old turning twenty-five face like a black veil, but couldn't hide the spark of intelligence in her brown eyes.

"It's past time to get up, sleepyhead. Where's Brandy?"

"She's still asleep," Gina mumbled, rubbing sleep from her world-weary eyes.

"Get her up and downstairs to day care,

and you hurry up. I don't want to hear any excuses about you being late for class. I expect to see you downstairs in a half hour. Understood?"

"Yes, Ms. Williams."

"Good. Now get moving before Ms. Betsy catches me."

Gina giggled. "Okay."

Dione turned away, smiling. Gina had potential. She could see it in her school-work, in her conversation. Gina had a future that Dione didn't want to see her lose because of having a baby too young. She just needed someone to remind her that she was worthy and worthwhile. They all did.

Walking down the hall and then upstairs to the third floor, Denise and her two-year-old son Mahlik were on their way down, followed by Kisha who carried her six-month-old daughter Anayshia in her arms.

From the moment Kisha moved into the residence, three months earlier, she and Denise were inseparable. It was like watching a modern-day miracle. The once recalcitrant and hostile Denise began to bloom, watered and fed by Kisha's friendship and outgoing personality.

"Good morning ladies, and gentleman," Dione greeted, bending to give Mahlik a quick kiss on the cheek.

"Mornin', Ms. Williams," they chorused.

Dione took a peek inside the pink bundle in Kisha's arms. "How is Anayshia feeling?"

"Much better. I took her to the doctor like you said and I've been giving her the new formula."

"So it was the formula that was making her sick?"

Kisha nodded. "Just like you said, Ms. Williams." She grinned. "You should have been a doctor."

"I don't think so." She smiled. "But I've seen the symptoms enough. My daughter was allergic to her formula when she was a baby, too."

"I didn't know you had a daughter, Ms. Williams."

"Sure do. Almost eighteen years old. She's away at college."

"Wow. How old does that make you?" Kisha quizzed.

Dione put her hand on her hip. "Old enough not to have to answer. Now get moving all four of you."

"Bye, Ms. Williams," they chimed as they brushed by her and down the stairs.

Dione shook her head and smiled. "How old am I? Ha."

She continued up to the top floor, making certain that everyone was up and about, then headed back downstairs. It was her regular routine and she had yet to grow tired of it.

Brenda was right, she thought, making her way down. This was hers, her baby. She'd given birth to Chances Are as sure as she'd given birth to Niyah. She loved and nurtured the girls and their children who came through her doors seeking help, the same way she'd finally found the love she'd needed.

A shudder of remembrance ran through her every time she thought about those lonely, frightening, difficult days when she'd wandered the streets after school and slept on the trains at night, sneaking into the girls' bathroom at school first thing in the morning to wash up and brush her hair. She'd stashed her suitcase in her locker and changed clothes every day before class started. On Fridays she'd take the suitcase out of the locker and wash her clothes at the laundry, bringing the clothes back on Monday. If anyone asked why she always had a suitcase, she told them she was staying with her cousin on the weekends.

For nearly a month, she'd drifted through life not sure how, just by pure willpower. She could barely stay awake in class and constantly felt sick. She wasn't sure how

Ms. Langley, the guidance counselor, found out about her secret life, but she did and called her into her office.

"Please close the door, Dione and have a seat," Ms. Langley said.

Reluctantly, Dione did as she was told, tried to smile and act nonchalant even as her stomach roiled and her heart bounced around in her chest.

"Is there anything you want to tell me, Dione?"

"No," she muttered.

"Then I'll start." Ms. Langley folded her hands on the desktop and leaned forward. "I think you're in trouble, Dione, and so do your teachers. We've all noticed the difference in your appearance, your mood and your classwork. If you'll talk to me about what's wrong I can help you, or talk to your parents for you if you want."

Dione violently shook her head. "No!"

"I want to help you, Dione." She came around the desk and put her arm around Dione's shoulders, and the dam burst.

"Good morning, Dee."

Dione blinked, shutting out the images of the past. "Good morning, Ms. Betsy."

Betsy stepped out the door of her ground floor apartment. "I know you were up there checking on that lazy Gina," she grumbled, wagging an accusing finger at Dione.

Dione tried not to look guilty. "I was checking on everybody."

Betsy pursed her lips, then sucked her teeth. "You gotta get these young girls to stand on their own feet. Be responsible. What are they gonna do when they have to step out into the real world without you there to keep them under your wings?"

A surge of heartsickness swept through her. "I don't even want to think about it, Ms. Betsy. You know how hard it is for me to let them go. They're just babies themselves. And —"

"You're not your mother, Dione. You're gettin' them ready for life, not throwing them out onto the street." Betsy wagged her finger again. "You were just as young as these girls when —"

"Yes. But I had you."

Betsy clucked her tongue and patted Dione's arm. "I have work to do," she fussed. "I know my early birds Denise and Kisha are waiting on me to take those babies so they can get to school."

Dione grinned. "You have a good day." She kissed the older woman's cheek before they parted, a ritual that began nearly eighteen years earlier, when Betsy was her landlady for the rooming house she and her infant daughter Niyah lived in.

She remembered walking for what seemed like forever to find that building. Ms. Langley had given her the address after she'd spent a week in a shelter and refused to go back. She'd had to sleep on a cot with a mattress no thicker than the thin blanket that covered her. She heard things — noises in the night and the soft sobs of the young women around her. The second day she was there she'd awakened to find most of her clothes missing and five dollars out of her wallet. When she arrived at school with what she had on her back and stormed teary-eyed into Ms. Langley's office, she swore she'd kill herself if she ever had to go back.

Ms. Langley jumped up and shut the door. "Dione, what happened?" Her green eyes raced across Dione's ravaged face and body to assess if there was any damage.

"I'm not going back there, Ms. Langley. I won't."

"Dione, you can't live on the street. You're going to have that baby in two months. You have to have someplace to live."

"I'll live on the street if I have to. I did it before. But I can't go back there, and you can't make me go."

"Yes, I can, Dione. By law you're still a minor. I should have had you placed in foster care instead of sending you there."

Dione looked at her defiantly. "You can't send me anywhere I don't want to go. Nobody can. I'm eighteen." Her eyes filled and she felt her throat constrict. "Today's my birthday."

It was Betsy who cared for Niyah while Dione returned to finish high school, and worked part-time at the local supermarket three days per week after giving birth to her baby girl. And Betsy always made sure that when Dione dragged herself home after her long days at school and then at work, there was a meal for her to eat.

Humph, that building. It was an old, rag-gedy building that was hotter than Hades in the summer and could rival the Arctic in the winter, located smack in the middle of the notorious East New York section of Brooklyn, one of the most dangerous areas of the borough. But it was inexpensive. The only thing she could afford. The check she received from Public Assistance for her and Niyah and the small salary she earned at the supermarket just about made ends meet.

One thing she was always grateful for, Ms. Betsy was real careful about choosing her six tenants, so Dione always felt safe, and Betsy seemed to have taken an instant lik-ing to her and Niyah. She always went out of her way to make sure that they had enough to eat and extra blankets during the bitter winter nights.

When Dione graduated from high school, it was Betsy who sat in the audience cheering for her, with Niyah squirming on her lap.

Dione promised herself that if — no, when — she made a success of her life she would get Ms. Betsy out of that building and take care of her the same way she had taken care of her and Niyah. And Dione had kept her promise. She smiled as she walked toward the main office. Yes she had.

When Dione entered the office, Brenda was busy pulling files that were scheduled for the monthly review.

This was one of the aspects of the job that was a mixture of triumph and disappointment. When the girls' progress files were brought before the staff for review, Dione always believed that the results, whatever they may be, were a direct reflection on the staff and the program, and ultimately on her.

If the girls were unable to achieve the goals set out for them, Dione felt the staff should have done more, *she* should have done more. The comprehensive program that she'd developed for the residents relied on all of the pieces working together: continuing education, finding employment, attending onsite housing preparation classes that taught budgeting, cooking, housekeeping and parenting skills.

In the five years since the house had been opened, thirty young women and their children had come through the doors and lived under that roof. Most of them took the opportunity, love and support that was give them and multiplied it when they went out on their own. But there were those who were beyond saving. The ones who'd come to her too late, too damaged by life. The ones who kept her awake on so many nights.

She pushed the thoughts aside as she crossed the rectangular room. "What time is the case review meeting scheduled for?"

Brenda looked briefly over her shoulder. "Four-thirty."

Dione nodded. "What about the house meeting?"

"I'll draft up the notice and have it under everyone's door. The proposal is on your desk downstairs."

"Thanks." She turned to leave, then stopped. "Bren?"

"Hmm?"

"Do you really think this documentary is

the way to go?" She folded her arms and leaned against the door frame.

Brenda laid down the file and faced Dione. "We've pretty much run out of options. The proposal sounds good and if marketed properly could get us the financing we need. That's what we have to focus on." She waited a beat, looking at Dione's faraway expression. "What's really bothering you, Dee? I don't think it's just the girls."

Dione straightened. "Why would you think that? Of course that's all there is. I don't want them exploited."

Brenda looked at Dione for a long moment. "If you say so." She turned back to the file cabinet.

"I'll be downstairs if you need me."

"Sure," Brenda mumbled.

Dione returned to her basement office, leaving the door partially open. Even though Brenda and Ms. Betsy had insisted that she close her door while she was working, Dione never wanted any of the girls to feel that she was inaccessible. Her steadfast policy interrupted many a thought process, but she stood by it.

She turned on the small lavender and white clock radio that was given to her as a gift from one of the former residents the previous Christmas. As the sultry sounds of Regina Bell overcame the static and filled the room, she thought about the question Brenda asked.

How could she tell Brenda that yes, she was right, the girls' privacy wasn't all that she was concerned with. She was concerned with her own privacy and what the probing of this documentary may uncover, that the lie she'd woven for the past eighteen years would become unraveled.

That's what she didn't want to risk, hurting Niyah with the truth. But at what cost?

She blew out a breath and opened the folder that contained the proposal. G.L. Productions stared back at her in thick, black capital letters. A tiny jolt shot through her. She wasn't sure why. Blinking, she turned the page and began reviewing what G.L. Productions had proposed to do in order to fulfill the requirements of the granting agency.

According to what Mr. Lawrence wrote, his intention was to get personal interviews with some of the residents and ask them all about their backgrounds and how they found themselves at Chances Are. She wrinkled her nose and shook her head. "That's out."

She continued to read, becoming more

agitated by the minute. She was right when her first thought told her to scrap the whole documentary idea. Not only did they want to interview all of the girls, but the staff as well. They also wanted to take footage of the activities in the house. And with the girls' permission, get interviews from any family members. *She couldn't see that happening.*

Closing the folder, Dione leaned back in her chair and rubbed her eyes with the tips of her index fingers. She'd only given the proposal a cursory glance when it had come in two months earlier and dismissed it as something she had no intention of participating in. But after a careful review, she had even more doubts than before. Only now, the dire situation at Chances had escalated.

Well, she conceded, if she was going to go through with it, as she was feeling compelled to do, she'd have to outline her own set of requirements. But she'd let the girls decide at the house meeting.

CHAPTER 2

Garrett Lawrence sat in the tight editing suite of his production studio, facing three television monitors, the video player and recording decks, putting together the final touches on an instructional video for a collection agency. The piece was well done, all of the important points were highlighted with animated graphics over narration. He knew the client would be pleased with the finished product — and he was bored. He wanted a project he could really sink his teeth into, something that had meaning, substance.

When he'd opened his production company four years earlier, he saw himself as the next Spike Lee, doing important, controversial work. The day had yet to arrive. It had taken all of his savings and a major bank loan to get G.L. Productions up and operational. For a small facility, it had all the latest in digital equipment and could easily compete with the bigger houses if it had the chance. But a small, black company already had two strikes against it right from the starting gate. *Small* and *black.*

If he could only get that Williams woman to accept the proposal, he knew that would be his ticket. Although, he had to admit that wasn't his thought two months earlier. But now he had thirty days to get her to agree, or he would lose his grant, unless he could miraculously find another shelter for wayward girls that fit the grant criteria. And grants like this one were few and far between.

In the two months since he'd made his telephone pitch, which he followed with a formal letter and the outline of what he wanted to accomplish, he'd called several times to try to get an appointment, but he'd never been able to get past her assistant. He knew if he could sit down face-to-face with her, he could convince her to go for the project.

Garrett made an adjustment to the image on the screen. Who did she think she was anyway that she didn't even have to give him the courtesy of a reply?

Satisfied, he turned off the equipment and stood, stretching his arms above his head hoping to loosen the kinks from hours of sitting.

Chances Are. Hmm. Wonder where they came up with the name? Chances *were,* loose girls wound up in places like that, or worse. People needed to see that. See them for what they really were: a burden on society.

When the request for proposals from the funding agency had been sent out, he originally had no intention of going for a contract documenting the lives of teen mothers — glorifying them. The very idea resuscitated the anger and the hurt he struggled to keep buried every day. It was his business partner and best friend, Jason Burrell, who'd finally convinced him that with the money and the exposure, it was the ticket they needed to take the company to the next level. "Get away from this instructional BS and do something worthwhile," he'd said.

Reluctantly, Garrett had agreed. He knew it would be hard working with and talking to a group of females who epitomized everything he despised. But he knew Jason was right. So he did his research and found Chances Are, and wrote his proposal based on the premise that the director would agree to be filmed. Ha. So much for assuming.

"Hey, man. Whatsup?"

Garrett turned toward Jason who stood in the doorway. "Just finishing up the collection agency piece."

"Hmm, glad that's out of the way." Jason stepped into the room and straddled an available stool. "Hear anything from the shelter?"

"Naw. Not a word. She doesn't even have the decency to return our calls." He sneered. "Probably too busy trying to keep those girls out of trouble — again."

"I say we start looking elsewhere before we blow the grant, man. It's a lot of money to lose."

"Yeah, I've been tossing around the same idea. Problem is, the grant was real specific about what it wanted: a documentary on teen mothers living in a residential setting and how they got there. Chances Are is the only one of its kind not funded by the government. And we dug the hole deeper by detailing how we were going to do it."

"I hear ya. That does limit our choices. But we gotta make a move. And soon. You want me to try to call again? Maybe I'll get lucky and get past that guard-dog assistant of hers."

Garrett blew out a breath. "Let's give it another day or two. I'm going over to the

33

research library this afternoon, do some more hunting. Maybe *I'll* get lucky and find someplace else that meets the guidelines."

"I sure as hell hope so." Jason stood. "Well, I have a shoot at New York University. I'm gonna pack up the equipment and get rolling."

"Who's on the crew?"

"Najashi, Paul, and Tom."

Garrett nodded. "I'll probably see you in the morning, then. I'll lock up when I'm done in here. Make sure they give you our check before you guys leave."

"I'm getting the check *before* we start. I don't want to hear nothing about how 'the person with the check is gone for the day' after we've done the work."

Garrett chuckled recalling the many times they'd been stiffed and had to wait weeks, sometimes months, after a shoot to get paid.

"All right, I'm out. Good luck with your research."

"Yeah."

Garrett switched off the lights, checked the studio where they did their on-site shooting and the adjoining rooms, set the answering machine and the alarms and stepped outside to the lukewarm October afternoon. He stood in the doorway of his West Village office space and watched the passersby.

All up and down the avenue, folks strolled, stopped, peeked in antique shop windows, hugged, laughed. Everyone seemed to have somebody. Someone to experience and share their day with. He watched a young mother laughing with her son, then she bent down and picked him up and gave him a big hug before setting him back on his feet. The little boy looked up at her, a hundred-watt smile on his face.

A sudden, razor-sharp pain of hurt and betrayal sliced through his stomach. Why wasn't he good enough to be hugged and kissed from the mother who gave him life to the wife who left him for greener pastures?

His chest filled. His throat constricted. Most times he didn't think about those things. His work filled his days, and most of his nights. But this whole business with the documentary and the shelter brought back all the ugly memories. Hey, he'd get through it. He was tough. That's what he'd been told the doctors said when he'd been found only hours old, wrapped in a sheet, wedged between two garbage cans.

He swallowed. Yeah, he was tough.

CHAPTER 3

The last of the girls, accompanied by their infants or toddlers, filed into the basement, which had been transformed from the day-care setting to a formal meeting space, the cribs, bassinets and playpens replaced with folding aluminum chairs.

Everyone tried to find a seat next to their buddy, whispering and speculating among themselves about why they were there.

"They're probably going to tell us about the loud music again," Kisha whispered to Denise. "You know how Ms. Betsy is about music."

Denise sucked her teeth. "Pleeze. They wouldn't call an emergency house meeting just to tell us about no darn music."

"Betcha," Kisha insisted.

"Probably gonna tell us about curfew again," Gina said under her breath, knowing she was one of the culprits and hoping she wouldn't be singled out to have her visiting privileges suspended. She wanted to see her boyfriend on the weekend. But she'd come in late two nights last week and had her toes and fingers crossed that she'd gotten over this time. Her daughter Brandy began squirming and whimpering. Gina stuck a bottle in her mouth and began bouncing Brandy up and down on her knee.

"If everyone will settle down, we can get started," Brenda said from the front of the room. "If any of the babies are asleep, or you want to lay them down, take a sheet from the cabinet in the back and put them in one of the cribs or playpens."

She waited while two of the girls leaped at the opportunity to put their bundles down. Once they were seated she began again.

"We have some serious business to discuss tonight and I want all of you to listen carefully to what Ms. Williams has to say. It affects all of us." She turned to Dione, who moved from the side of the room and took Brenda's place in front of the girls.

"An opportunity has presented itself to us. But as Ms. Brenda said, your decision — and it will be your decision — affects everyone." She looked from one questioning face to the next before she continued. "A gentleman by the name of Garrett Lawrence would like to do a documentary, a short film, about you girls and Chances Are."

"A movie!" Kisha beamed.

"Something like that," Dione qualified.

A wave of murmuring rippled through the room.

"Okay, settle down. Nothing gets settled by talking among yourselves. It may sound exciting, but there are some other things to consider. He's going to want to interview all of you, and your faces will be on film. I have no guarantees about who will eventually see it."

Denise's hand shot up in the air. "I can't be on no film, Ms. Williams. I can't."

"Me, neither. None of my friends in school know I live in a shelter," said another girl in the back.

"Yeah. Yeah," chimed a few others.

"So don't be in it," snapped Kisha, looking behind her and giving the whiners dirty looks.

"Oh, shut up. It ain't all about you," snapped Theresa, one of the oldest in the group who'd been the victim of incest and held a blatant distrust of everyone and everything. It had taken Dione months to be able to get her to talk at all. The last thing she wanted for Theresa was a setback.

Kisha jumped up out of her seat, squaring

off for a fight. She was always ready to defend herself or somebody and she was the smallest one in the bunch.

"Kisha! Sit down. Now!" Dione ordered.

Kisha blew out a breath and took her seat.

"Now just settle down. Everybody. Nothing is going to happen without everyone's cooperation. I know this is a very sensitive issue for many of you. And you know that I've always done everything in my power to keep your privacy intact. We'll put it to a vote." She looked around the room. "All those in favor of the film being done, raise your hand."

Four hands shot up in the air, leaving the majority of six in disagreement.

Dione sighed, partly in relief, partly in disappointment. "That's it then. No film."

There was a sudden outburst of conversation among the opposing sides, everyone trying to outshout the other.

"Quiet! Enough. End of discussion." By degrees everyone settled down. "Thank you all for coming. The meeting is over."

There was a lot of scraping of chairs and loud murmurs as the girls started to get up.

"Wait a minute." Brenda stepped to the front of the room, her face a mask of barely contained fury.

Dione put her hand on Brenda's shoulder

in warning.

"No. They need to hear what I have to say," she whispered.

She turned toward the assemblage. "Everybody take a seat." She waited, tapping her foot with impatience. "I can understand some of you being reluctant about the whole thing for a variety of reasons. Ms. Williams didn't tell you all everything, but I will." She cut Dione a quick look from the corner of her eye and could see that Dione was fuming but resigned. "This is the real deal . . ."

Brenda told them plainly and slowly about the financial troubles Chances Are was in, and how making the documentary and getting it to important funders could be the key to saving the house.

"From the moment each of you walked through the doors, we have gone out of our way to make a home for you, help you in any way we could, get your lives and your children's lives back on track. I think it's about time you all began thinking about more than just yourselves and just today, but all the tomorrows and all the young women who will need Chances Are when you've moved out and moved on." She took a breath. "I want you all to think about this. Think about it real hard." She turned away and walked out, leaving them all in open-mouthed silence.

Dione found Brenda in the upstairs office, with the lights out, sitting in a chair by the window, her silhouette reflected against the moonlit night.

"Bren." Dione heard her sniffle.

"Yeah," she mumbled.

Dione stepped into the room. "Can I turn on the light?"

"I'd really prefer if you didn't."

Dione walked over to where Brenda sat and put a hand on her shoulder. "I think you really shook them up down there," she began trying to get a chuckle out of her.

"I had to. They need to know the truth, Dee." She sniffed again. "Our hearts and souls are in this place."

"I know. We'll find a way, Bren. Work on some more proposals, do some fund-raising. I'm not giving up."

Brenda clasped the hand on her shoulder. "I'm sorry. I know you didn't want them to know how bad things really were. But —"

"It's all right. You were right. They do need to know. It's not fair to them to leave them in the dark. The reality is, if we can't get some funding in here, we'll have to start looking for placement for them."

Brenda sighed. "I'm not looking forward to that, but it's a reality."

Dione squeezed her shoulder. "Something will work out. Go home and get some rest. I'll see you in the morning."

"Yeah." Slowly she rose and Dione could see her wiping her eyes in the shadowed room.

They both got their coats from the closet and walked out together to the front door.

Just as they reached the exit, Kisha came running down the stairs.

"Ms. Williams, Ms. Frazier. Wait!"

They both turned, fearing the worst, like a fight broke out upstairs or something.

"What's the matter, Kisha?" Dione asked, holding her breath.

Kisha came to a stop in front of them. "We took another vote. We can't let you lose Chances Are, Ms. Williams. It ain't right."

"Isn't," Dione corrected with a smile.

"Isn't. But we want to help."

Brenda turned to Dione and a smile broke out across her face. She grabbed Dione and hugged her. "Amen!"

Dione hugged her back as fear whipped through her. The racing of her heart had nothing to do with happiness.

That night Dione tossed and turned, her

life, her youth, her lie tracking her like the most skilled of hunters. Everywhere that she tried to hide from the painful memories — there they were.

She ran, darting behind her successes, her degrees, her small cluster of friends, the security of Chances Are, but still the memories sought her out and found her. All in the form of Niyah who held out the accusing finger. "How could you have done it — lied to me all these years? I hate you," she screamed. "Hate you!"

CHAPTER 4

When Garrett arrived at the studio the following morning Jason was already there setting up to shoot a public service announcement for the local historical society.

Garrett poked his head in. "Hey, how's it going?"

"I should be asking you," he said adjusting the teleprompter for the woman from the society.

"No luck if that's what you mean."

Jason stopped what he was doing. " 'Scuse me a minute," he said to the woman seated in front of the monitor. He crossed the studio floor to where Garrett stood in the doorway. "I'm telling you, man, call her. Lay the cards on the table. Just be upfront," he said under his breath.

"Listen, I ain't begging nobody for nothing. We got this far without this project, we'll keep going."

"Yeah, doing the same thing day in and

day out," he hissed. "What about our plans, man? Huh?"

"Listen, Jas. If we could get one grant, we'll get another. I'm not going to sweat this. If she decides to call and accept, fine. If not we'll move on."

Jason tossed it around a minute and looked long and hard at his friend, knowing that once Garrett made up his mind on something that was it. "Yeah, all right, man. You're the boss. Whatever you decide to do I'm behind you." He slapped him on the shoulder. "Just don't take too long to think up something brilliant."

Garrett chuckled. "Yeah, right. Thanks. No pressure. See you later. I'll be in editing. Tom and Najashi in yet?"

"Tom is. Najashi should be here around noon."

"Cool. Later."

Dione had alternately been staring at the phone then at the proposal. Debating. Yes, the girls had rethought the idea and had decided to go along with it. But what about her? She felt as if she were being squeezed like a lemon. There was no easy win. Either way she stood to lose a lot.

All during her restless night, she thought about her options, and her level of participation. The bottom line was she only had to reveal as much or as little as she wanted. Niyah didn't have to find out how ugly her beginnings really were.

Resigned, she reached for the phone, just as it rang.

"Good morning, Chances Are. Ms. Williams speaking."

"Hey, Dee, it's Terri."

Dione's face and spirit instantly brightened at hearing the voice of her dear friend Terri Powers.

"Girl, it's good to hear your voice," she enthused, easily slipping into the sistah mode. "When did you sneak back into town?"

"Just got in last night," she said with her barely there Barbadian accent. "Clint and I were overdue for a vacation. We've been burning the candle at both ends."

"Yeah, I hear you. But it's always extra nice when you have your own getaway resort to get away to."

They both laughed. Terri's husband, Clint, had opened a small resort several years earlier in the Bahamas and it had really taken off. Between Clint's uncanny business skills and Terri's public relations savvy, their careers and their finances were set. They'd gone through hell and back before finally getting together; from the kidnapping of Clint's daughter, Ashley, to the resurrection of Terri's brother, Malcolm, who she'd believed had been dead for years — but they did get together and they were exceedingly happy.

"So, what's been happening? Any luck with the proposals?"

"No," she pushed out a long breath. "But we've finally decided to go with the documentary."

"Fantastic! I told you weeks ago it was a great idea. You know I'd be more than thrilled to put a promo campaign together for you once it's done. No problem."

Dione smiled. "I'm going to hold you to that. We'll need all the help we can get."

"If you hadn't wanted to carry the weight of that place on your shoulders, I told you I would have worked out a P.R. campaign for you to pitch to those stuck-up funders."

"I know, I know. Don't rub it in."

"When does it start?"

"That's the thing. I'm not sure. Actually, we just decided last night. We put it to a house vote. I haven't even spoken to the producer yet. He may not want to do it at this point."

"He'll do it. The story behind Chances Are is a gem. Your story especially."

Dione's stomach fluttered. "That's my biggest concern, Terri. You know that. Niyah doesn't know everything."

"Dee, it's time that she did. She's almost eighteen."

"I know," she said, a sad hitch in her voice. "I just don't ever want her to feel the same worthlessness that I felt for so many years. Or that my bringing her into the world was the cause of —"

"Don't even go there. If anything, Niyah was and still is the catalyst for everything that you've become. Everything that you've done for so many other young girls who had no one and nowhere else to turn. That's something to be proud of, Dee, not ashamed."

"And how many times over the years have I had this very conversation with myself? It's just easier said than done."

"Well, sister-friend, it's got to come out sometime."

"That's what I'm afraid of. But I'll work it out."

"You always do. Now make that call, girl. I'm itching for a new project."

Dione laughed. "I will and I'll call and let you know what happens."

"Good luck."

"Thanks, Terri. Talk to you soon."

Slowly Dione replaced the receiver, a soft smile framing her mouth. She was blessed. That was certain. She was surrounded by people who cared for and believed in her. And they were depending on her. How would her life have been different if her parents had been there for her when she needed them most?

She took a long breath, picked up the phone and dialed Garrett Lawrence's number.

Garrett was right in the middle of putting the crucial piece of a choreographer's video together. Painstakingly he ran and reran the tape to get it in perfect sync with the music.

At first he ignored the ringing phone, intent on what he was doing, until he realized that everyone else was in the studio taping the pubic service announcement.

"Man!" He stopped the tape, silently promising himself for the millionth time to set the answering machine for those days when Marva, their part-time receptionist, was off. He snatched the phone from its base on the wall behind him.

"Hello," he barked. "G.L. Productions."

Dione frowned at the abrasive voice on the other end and hoped that whoever this was, wasn't representative of who she'd have to deal with.

"Yes. Good morning. This is Dione Williams from Chances Are. May I speak with Mr. Lawrence please?"

Garrett sat straight up in his seat, the video forgotten, partly from the jolt of the call itself, but mostly from the throaty, almost hushed voice of the caller.

"This is Garrett Lawrence. How are you, Ms. Williams?"

Now that's more like it. "Fine. I'm calling because I've gone over your proposal again — and," she forced the words out of her mouth, "I'd like to set up a time when we can meet to discuss the arrangements. That is if you're still interested in working with us."

"Yes, I'm still interested," he said, fighting to hold back his enthusiasm. "Whatever time is good for you. I'll make myself available."

She was hoping he'd say it was too late, but — "How's this afternoon, about four o'clock?"

"Four is fine. I'll be there."

"No. I mean, actually I'd prefer if we met somewhere else."

It was his turn to frown. He would have thought she'd want to meet on her turf. *Women.* "You're welcome to come to the studio. That would give you a chance to see the facility and I can show you some of the work I've done."

"All right. What's the best way to get there by car?"

The morning sped by entirely too quickly. Before Dione knew it, it was three o'clock and if she had any intention of being on time, she needed to leave. She'd put off the inevitable for as long as possible.

Dione signed off on the last case file. Overall she was pleased with the reviews of the girls' progress. Her staff meeting the previous afternoon had yielded glowing remarks for the ten residents. Only two out of the ten were in need of new physicals, and appointments had been set up.

Everyone with the exception of Theresa was either in school or working. According to her files from the group home she'd been transferred from, she hadn't gone any further than seventh grade and had been diagnosed as a "special ed" student.

However, in the three months that she'd been at Chances Are, the staff had determined that Theresa's problem was dyslexia, which was never properly diagnosed or treated. Brenda had investigated several special programs and they'd finally found one that would be perfect for Theresa. Now the only problem they faced was convincing Theresa that she could succeed in school and in life — with a little help and hard work.

Dione closed Theresa's file and put it with the stack to be returned to the cabinet. Getting up, she took her purse and coat from the coatrack and headed upstairs.

She peeked in the door of the main office. "I'm going to the meeting with Mr. Lawrence," she said to Brenda.

"I can go with you if you want."

Dione smiled. "No. Thanks. I'll deal with it. See you in the morning." She turned to leave.

"Keep an open mind, Dee," Brenda called out.

"Yeah, yeah. I will."

"Why did she decide to come here?" Jason asked.

"That's the way she wanted it and I wasn't going to debate the point."

They walked side by side through the facility checking each of the rooms, wanting to make a good impression, then returned to the front office.

"I'd like you to sit in on the meeting, Jason. Fill in anything I might overlook."

"No problem."

Garrett checked his watch. "She should be here in a few minutes. We have anybody to cover the phones while we meet?"

"I'll get Najashi or Tom. Whoever's not busy."

The front door buzzed.

Jason looked at the security monitor mounted on the office wall. "Mmm, if this is her, we're in luck buddy." He buzzed her in.

Garrett just shook his head, knowing that Jason thought any woman with a grain of looks was fair game, even though he was solidly married. So his assessment could often leave a lot to be desired.

They could hear her heels click down the hall.

Garrett stepped out of the office into the corridor to meet her.

"You're on," Jason whispered.

Garrett stopped, watching her approach and was immediately reminded of those sleek Ebony Fashion Fair models strutting down a runway.

She wore a full-length cream-colored cashmere coat that she'd left open to showcase a body-hugging jersey knit turtleneck dress. Her auburn hair barely brushed her shoulders and was swept away from her face. Dark glasses shielded her eyes and when she removed them, startling hazel eyes zeroed in on him, set against a rich tan complexion devoid of any noticeable makeup, save for a hint of cinnamon-colored lipstick.

His stomach seesawed. He wasn't sure what he'd been expecting, but it wasn't this vision. Somewhere in his subconscious he'd convinced himself that anyone who ran a home for girls was a short nondescript plain-Jane, who couldn't get a man, even if they did have a great voice on the phone.

He swallowed and a sudden heat swept through him when the sexiest smile he'd seen in far too long slowly slid across her mouth.

And then she was right in front of him, her hand outstretched.

"I'm Dione Williams. I'm here to see —"

"Me. I'm Garrett Lawrence." He took her hand and had the overwhelming urge to caress it instead of shake it. *Get it together, brother.* "Good to finally meet you, Ms. Williams. Come in. I'd like to introduce you to my business partner." He released her hand and Dione inexplicably felt adrift.

While she was walking down the corridor and had seen him standing there, her first thought was that he was an actor, or something, here to do a taping. Never in her wildest dreams did she associate this delicious-looking man with the voice on the phone. Garrett Lawrence was a work of art in motion.

The tight black sweater outlined the breadth of his shoulders and defined the hard contours of his upper body. The pale blue jeans he wore — well, they set her imagination into high gear.

She couldn't remember the last time simply meeting a man had this kind of powerful effect on her. *There had to be something wrong with him.* And then he turned and smiled, flashing the deep dimple in his right cheek and the sexy gap in his front teeth.

It was hot. Too hot. She needed to get out of her coat.

"Ms. Williams, this is my business partner Jason Burrell."

Jason stood and extended his hand. "Nice to meet you, Ms. Williams."

Dione gave him a tight smile, trying to give herself a minute to recoup. "You, too."

"Can I take your coat?" Garrett stepped behind her and helped her with her coat.

A shiver raced up her spine when his fingers brushed her back, and the subtle scent that he wore, wafted around her, light as a breeze.

"Have a seat. Make yourself comfortable," Jason said, indicating a chair at the circular conference table.

"Thank you." Dione slipped her glasses in her purse and sat down, crossing her long legs at the knee.

Garrett and Jason took the two remaining chairs and tried to keep their eyes off her legs.

"I hope you don't mind if Jason sits in on the meeting," Garrett stated more than asked.

"Not at all." Now she wished she had brought Brenda along. At least between the two of them, one would have been able to pay attention to what was being said and not the timbre of Garrett's voice or the brilliance of his dimpled smile.

"Good." He blew out a breath and folded his hands on the table. "I know you probably have a lot of questions about the proposal, so why don't you start."

Now she was in her element. She could focus on what she'd come to say and not how he kept making her stomach jump up and down every time he looked in her direction. She cleared her throat. "Not so much questions," she began in that low-down voice that shimmied in the air then settled in the center of his belly and vibrated. "More like guidelines."

"Fine. Let's hear them."

Item by item she went down a laundry list of "do nots."

"The outside of the building can never be filmed at any time. I have to ensure their privacy and in some instances their safety. None of the girls can be filmed or interviewed without a staff member present and they are not to be asked questions without being advised what they will be beforehand."

Minute by minute Garrett was becoming more annoyed. By the time she finished with her litany of what he couldn't do, he wouldn't have anything worth filming. Yet even with his anger rising to the surface like molten lava, ready to overflow and scorch everything in its path, he couldn't help but be fascinated by Dione. He could hear the intelligence, determination and fire in her voice. He could see the intensity and passion flame in her eyes, and feel the strength that radiated from her like an erotic scent, all mixed together in one incredible package.

So what made a woman like Dione Williams use all her intellect, beauty and strong will to work with a group of loose, moralless girls?

"Does that about cover everything, Ms. Williams?" Garrett asked when she'd finally concluded.

Jason shot him a look, knowing that Garrett was ready to bust, which Garrett totally ignored.

"There won't be much for us to shoot," he added.

She could see his smile was forced, but he couldn't hide that dimple if he tried. *Stay focused, girl.* "I'm sure if you're as skilled as you claim in your proposal you'll find enough for your film." She angled her chin in a challenge.

Hmm. He liked that. She didn't back down. There was obviously no compromise with this one.

Garrett leaned forward, his voice dropped to a new low. "Believe me, Ms. Williams, I *am* as good as I say."

She suddenly felt as if a raging furnace door had been opened and she was standing right in front. His comment was purely casual, it was the tone and the swift, dark look in his eyes that rocked her to the core.

She gave him a cursory smile. "We'll have to see now, won't we?" She stood. "May I have that tour now?"

"Sure." He stood up. "Follow me."

"Oh, I'll just cover things until you get back," Jason said, giving Garrett a wink on the side. "Nice meeting you, Ms. Williams. Looking forward to working with you." He handed her her coat, which she draped over her arm.

Dione extended her hand and smiled. "Nice meeting you, also."

Garrett and Dione stepped out into the corridor and across the hall. "A couple of my crew members are shooting a PSA — a public service announcement — in the main studio."

"How many do you have — studios?" she asked as they walked into the control room and stood in the doorway.

"Two. The second one is down the hall."

She watched the three monitors in the control room while the woman on the screen told whoever cared to listen why they should make a donation to the historical society.

"That's Najashi," he whispered not wanting to disturb them, as he pointed to a man in all black with the short twists in his hair. "And that's Tom on the end working the audio."

The first thing she noticed about Tom was the tattoo of a snake that peeked out from the collar of his oversized Tommy Hilfiger shirt.

"Come on, I'll show you where the real work is done."

He took her into the editing room, closed the door and dimmed the lights. Dione's pulse quickened. Her body and mind went on full alert.

Garrett didn't even notice her agitation. Once in the dimly lit editing room, *he* was in his element, explaining the different machines and lighted dials, what they did and how a program was put together from raw footage.

"Sometimes it can take hours just to put five minutes worth of usable footage together. But it's the key to making the work look good."

On the monitors, he showed her some of the projects he'd worked on and what each one was about.

As she listened to him talk, her tension slowly began to ebb. She could tell that he loved and believed in what he did, and he probably was just as good as he claimed. She had to admit she liked listening to the deep resonance of his voice when he spoke, watching the cool control of his long fingers as he demonstrated how the equipment worked and the way he took his time and answered her myriad questions about what each machine did and how without making her feel silly.

It was fascinating. And so was Garrett Lawrence.

"That's about it for the dog and pony show," he said switching off the tape and turning to her in the black swivel chair.

There was that nice smile again.

"Very nice," she said in her best, I-don't-impress-easily voice.

His smile didn't waver. *She's a tough one.*

"How long do you think our, I mean the documentary project will take to complete?"

Oh, I heard that one. You're not as cool as you'd like me to think. "Hmm. If we get started within the next week, hopefully before Christmas."

"Christmas! But I need — I mean, why will it take so long? The whole point in my agreeing was to . . . get this over and done with as quickly as possible. I don't want your filming to interrupt the girls' holidays." She'd be damned if she'd tell him that Chances Are was in financial trouble and it needed this documentary to appeal to funders.

"Is interrupting the holidays another no-no that you forgot to mention?" He hated the holiday season. It always reminded

61

him of what he'd never had. So he always made it a point of working right through them. Kept his mind off himself. After so many years he rarely thought of what it meant to others and didn't care to know.

Her eyes widened and she was just about to open her mouth when Garrett held up his hand. "Listen, like I said before, the whole process takes time. We both want a great piece of work. Now I can come in and do something half-assed — excuse me, I mean — no, that's exactly what I mean." His eyes narrowed. "Or I can do what I know I can do — a fantastic job that everyone can be proud of. It's your choice."

He leaned back in his seat, angled his head to the right and folded his arms.

Three months, she thought. That would barely give her enough time to resubmit any proposal before the end of the year. And then an idea began to emerge.

"Mr. Lawrence, how successful are those PSA things?"

He shrugged. "They get people's attention if they're positioned right. Some of my clients swear by them."

"Do you think you could do some for me — for Chances Are while you work on the documentary?"

"Sure, I don't see why not."

She blew out a sigh of relief. Maybe she could get Terri to work out a publicity plan and use the PSA along with it. "When can we get started?"

Her excitement over the possibility sparkled in her eyes, Garrett noticed. "Whenever you're ready." He shrugged. "Tomorrow?"

She laughed. "How about next week?"

He liked the way she laughed, soft, but from deep inside. "Next week is fine. I'll check our schedule before you leave and give you a date. Do you want to do it here or at your place?"

She knew what he was asking, but the question still sounded so provocative. "What do you think would be best?"

"We can do one of each. And a combination of both." He grinned, slow and easy.

Her heart fluttered. "Great."

"But in the meantime, fair is fair, Ms. Williams. I showed you mine, when will you show me yours?"

Oh, these word games. The corner of her mouth curved up. "Call my office in the morning. I'll make arrangements."

"I'll do that." His gaze held hers.

She took a breath. "I'd better be going."

He took her coat from her arm and helped her to put it on.

She could have sworn he was standing a bit too close, especially when she felt his warm breath run along the back of her neck.

"Thank you," she mumbled.

"I'll walk you out."

When they reached the front door, she turned to him. "Thank you for a very informative afternoon."

"No problem."

They stood there looking at each other seeming not to know what to do next.

Dione swallowed. "I'll expect your call in the morning."

"First thing. But until then, don't keep me in suspense. Who's going to be your on-air personality for the PSA?"

She smiled. "Me."

His gaze rolled over her then back up to her eyes. The right corner of his mouth curved and his eyebrows arched. "Ever been in front of a camera before, Ms. Williams?"

"No. But I'm certain you'll make sure it doesn't look that way." She turned and walked toward her car.

"It will be my pleasure," he whispered, as he watched her slip behind the steering wheel. "It certainly will."

CHAPTER 5

Dione arrived at work the following morning before anyone in the house had even gotten up for the day. It was barely seven-thirty and she'd been through the building twice. Checking. She wanted to be sure that everything was in place, that Garrett Lawrence could find no fault with her domain. She couldn't put on a sideshow the way he had done, but she could certainly show him that she ran *her* facility with the same amount of care and attention to detail that he did. To her, finding fault with Chances Are was like finding fault with her. And for reasons that she didn't want to admit, it mattered more than usual that Garrett Lawrence saw nothing but perfection.

When the phone rang at seven forty-five, her heart jumped. She picked up on the second ring.

"Good morning. Chances Are. Ms. Williams speaking."

"Good morning." He was pleasantly surprised to hear her voice. He hadn't expected her to be there. Did she live there, too? "Hope I'm not calling too early. But I'm an early riser. This is Garrett Lawrence."

There was no need for him to identify himself. She'd heard that voice of his in her dreams. "Not at all. I've been here for a while."

Answers that question. "Just calling to confirm about today — for the visit. I thought about ten. If that's good for you."

"Ten is fine. Things should be calmed down by then."

"Calmed down?"

She laughed lightly. "What I mean is, chaos reigns supreme from about seven-thirty to nine, when everyone is rushing around trying to get ready for school, or work and getting the children that stay on-site down to childcare."

He frowned. "They go to school and work?" the incongruity of the idea momentarily stumbling his thinking.

She heard the disbelief in his voice and although she was used to it in most others, in Garrett she was disappointed.

"Of course. That's just one of the many criteria we have for the girls staying here."

"Hmm."

He almost sounded as if he thought she were lying. Now she really was annoyed. "Is there a problem, Mr. Lawrence?" she asked, snapping him to attention.

"No. Not at all."

"Then I'll see you at ten."

"Yes. Definitely."

"Goodbye." She hung up the phone, then stared at it for a few minutes. "I know what you're thinking, Mr. Lawrence. Well your thoughts are just about to be changed."

"I thought I heard somebody moving around. What in the world are you doing here so early?" Betsy shuffled into the room, still dressed in her nightgown and robe.

"I had a lot I wanted to get out of the way before everyone was up and about."

"Mmm. It must have kept you up last night to get you in here this early." She yawned. "Anything I can help you with?"

"No. But I just want to let you know that the producer will be here today to take a tour of the building."

Betsy straightened, fully awake. "Why didn't you say so? I got to get these lazy girls up and together. Make sure their apartments are up to par. You know how they can leave their places sometime when they run outta here in the morning."

"Maybe you can select one or two apartments for the visit and just let those girls know."

Betsy nodded. "That'll be easier. Kisha usually keeps a neat place, and Theresa."

"Perfect. And it'll be good for Theresa. Make her feel she's a part of things."

"I'll get them up right now and let them know." She turned away, then stopped. "So what's this man like?"

"Seems to know what he's doing."

"I sure hope so," she mumbled, moving away. "For these girls' sake. I sure do."

Dione blew out a breath. "So do I," she whispered, even as the memory of the tingle of his touch raised the hair on the back of her neck.

By the time Brenda arrived at eight, the building was virtually vibrating with energy. She could hear excited voices and footsteps darting across the hall above her head, and spotted several girls dashing up the staircase. She walked into the office while pulling off her coat, surprised to see Dione.

"Morning. What's going on? Feels like electric wires running through here. Betsy on another surprise inspection tear again?" She slid open the closet door, hung up her coat and sat down at her totally organized desk. She shifted her pencil cup to the center of the desk.

Dione smiled. "Something like that. Garrett Lawrence is stopping by this morning to take a tour. I wanted to make sure that everything was in order. He'll be taking a look at Kisha's and Theresa's apartments."

Brenda immediately noticed that Dione wouldn't look at her while she was talking, something very unusual for Dee. Brenda swiveled her chair fully in Dione's direction.

"So, the meeting went well."

"I think so." She shuffled some papers on the desk. "While I was there they were shooting a public service announcement for another organization. Mr. Lawrence said they work pretty well in getting attention. So I thought that we could do one and give it to my friend Terri, let her work up a promotional package for us."

"Sounds good to me. But what about the documentary?"

Dione explained about the length of time it would take to complete and her anxiety about not having enough time to resubmit the proposals.

Brenda blew out a breath and slowly shook her head of spiral curls. "If it's not one thing it's something else. But at least we'll have a shot with this public service thing."

"That's what I'm hoping."

Brenda looked at Dione's profile for a long moment, assessing the faraway look in her expression. Although they weren't what you would call best friends, and didn't share a lot of personal secrets, she felt she knew Dione well enough to sense when something was troubling her. But Dione had always been so self-contained, in control and focused. She seemed to have her life totally together. And even in the three years that she'd been working at Chances Are, Dione never shared her life story or why she decided to open the house. No more had ever been said beyond, "It's something I felt compelled to do. Someone had to do it."

Dione Williams was a private person. No one seemed to really know what drove her. What gave her the determination and drive. Maybe that's just the way she was. But Brenda had serious doubts that it was that simple. Something pushed Dione Williams. Whatever it was, it had one helluva hold on her.

"What time is this guy coming?"

"Ten." She fidgeted with the collar of her camel-colored silk blouse, then suddenly stood. "I'm going to check with Betsy. See how she's making out with the girls. It's time for day care to open."

Brenda watched her walk out and wondered again what was stirring beneath the cool-watered surface.

For the third time that morning, Dione inspected her building from top to bottom, finally stopping in the basement where day care was in full swing. *Sesame Street* was playing from the small, portable television, the soft scent of baby powder and sweet formula filled the air.

Betsy looked up from changing the diaper of one of the toddlers, seeing Dione standing in the doorway. Betsy set the baby boy down on the floor, gave him a light tap on his bottom and crossed the pale blue floor. She stopped directly in front of Dione, the top of her graying head just reaching Dione's chin. She stroked her cheek.

"What's wrong, chile? You got that haunted look in your eyes like when you was worrying over one thing or the other. Or about that baby girl of yours."

Dione forced a tight-lipped smile. "Just want to make sure everything is okay." She looked over Betsy's head, her eyes scanning the room.

"Of course everything is okay. Now, you want to tell me what's really bothering you, Dione Williams?"

Dione met Betsy's eyes. "I don't want

them to find any fault. We need this thing to work, Betsy." The little Betsy did know about their situation was enough. She didn't want to tell her just how desperate things were. That she hadn't taken a paycheck in more than a month, that she stayed up nights working and reworking the figures to make sure that the bills and the staff were paid, that the politicians were no longer interested in the plight of homeless young mothers, they had new agendas. How could she tell this to the woman whom she'd silently pledged to take care of?

"Of course it will. You just need to have a little faith."

"I'll keep that in mind. Did you make out okay with Kisha and Theresa?"

Betsy waved her hand in dismissal. "Those two were so excited, I almost couldn't get them out of here for school and Theresa off to that special reading test."

Dione smiled, then checked her watch. "I'd better get upstairs." She turned to go.

"I know something's bothering you, Dione," Betsy said, halting Dione's exit. "Let it go. Everything will work out. Always has."

Dione nodded, wanting to believe. But it had always been hard for her to have blind faith, ceaseless hope. She couldn't depend on the intangible things — things she couldn't see, couldn't touch. Hopes and dreams dissolved, like mist burned off after the morning sunrise. She couldn't trust emotion, only reality. Emotion got you in trouble. Made you stop thinking with your head. She couldn't afford that. Emotion had cost her once, she couldn't let it cost her again. Especially now.

Garrett slowed to a stop in front of the building and checked the address against the one written on the slip of paper. Frowning, he leaned closer to the passenger window and checked again. His gaze ran up and down the well-kept brownstone, the curtains and blinds that lined the oversized windows.

This couldn't be the place. Maybe he'd gotten the address wrong. But he was pretty sure he hadn't. This was a shelter? His vision of a shelter was nothing like what was in front of him. Probably just a front, he concluded. They couldn't very well have an eyesore in the center of this middle-class neighborhood. He was certain the inside would meet his expectations.

He shut off the car, took his portfolio from the passenger seat and got out.

By the time Dione reached the main floor,

she spotted Garrett through the glass-and-oak door, and was once again seized with a gentle wave of caressing heat, her earlier frustration soothed and massaged away.

She took a breath and unlocked the door, putting on her best, happy-to-see-you smile.

"Right on time," she greeted, stepping aside to let him pass. She caught a whiff of his cologne.

"That's just one of my many attributes." He gave her that dimpled smile and tugged off his Chicago Bulls baseball cap.

For a moment their gazes connected and Dione had the strangest feeling that he wasn't talking about his filming talents.

CHAPTER 6

Garrett followed Dione into the corridor, taking surreptitious glances around the interior, only to discover that the inside, at least as much of it as he could see, lived up to the outside.

But it was Dione who caught and commanded his attention. He hadn't stopped thinking about her since they'd met. He seemed to be able to hear the hushed timbre of her voice in his dreams. Her scent, so soft, subtle, yet intoxicating had stayed with him seeping into his pores. And now, the whisper of her stockings brushing against her long legs as she walked, the click of her heels and the gentle wave of her hips seemed to have him mesmerized. Why? He'd seen and been with plenty of women. What was it about her that intrigued him, sparked his curiosity?

"Let me take you to meet Brenda Frazier," she said, interrupting his meandering thoughts.

He blinked, bringing reality back into focus. He was in a well-kept building in a decent neighborhood, that appeared to be efficiently run. But the bottom line was, no matter what it looked like, no matter what window dressing you put on it, all it was, all it could ever be was a shelter for irresponsible girls and their illegitimate children. He had to remember that. Looks were deceiving.

He frowned as the old pain twisted in his chest. Did he really want this grant so badly that he was willing to deal with all the memories and the hurt that was certain to come with it? Maybe he should just let Jason take over the project.

"Brenda Frazier, this is Garrett Lawrence. Ms. Frazier is the assistant director of the facility."

Assistant director. Hmm. They'd thought she was just a pesky secretary, stonewalling them. If she was on a par with other assistant directors, she had some pull, some say-so about things. And from the no-nonsense look in her eyes, she was not one to be fooled with. You wanted her on your side.

Brenda came from behind her desk and extended her hand. "Pleasure to meet you."

"So you're the face behind the voice."

Brenda's smile was slow, almost wary. "I hope that's a good thing."

"Absolutely," he grinned, flashing those dimples. He turned toward Dione. "Ready for that tour?"

"We can start downstairs."

Dione took him down to day care, which doubled as their meeting room, which was full of the sounds of active children running, playing and wailing for attention. It took all Dione had not to burst out laughing when she introduced him to Betsy who all but batted her eyes at him. After a brief show-and-tell of the uses for the huge basement space, they went upstairs and he took a quick peek at Kisha's and Theresa's apartments.

"Are all the apartments like this?" he asked having a hard time believing that this was the type of environment the girls lived in. He felt like he was on a movie set that had been staged especially for him. Any moment now, someone would call "cut" and they'd take down the props and he'd see the skeletons in the closet.

Dione closed the door to Theresa's apartment. "Yes." She laughed lightly and he realized he liked the sound. "Some more well-kept than others, I'm sad to say. But they're all one bedroom, fully equipped and furnished when the families move in."

"Pretty lucky."

Dione snatched his sarcastic tone right out of the air and tossed it back at him. "I wouldn't call what these girls go through luck, Mr. Lawrence."

"What would you call it?" he taunted, suddenly feeling combative. "I mean, here they are, all their needs met, free room and board, built-in babysitter. Ha, it's almost as if they're being rewarded for going out and getting pregnant."

Dione's eyes flared and she could feel the heat of a nasty volley rise up from the pit of her stomach ready to jump up and smack him dead across his self-righteous face. How many times had she done battle with his type of twisted thinking? More times than she cared to count. Some battles she lost, but there were many more that she'd won. Education was the key and Mr. Garrett Lawrence was in serious need of Awakening 101, straight from the head teacher.

"It's unfortunate that you feel that way, Mr. Lawrence. I would think that as a *professional* you'd have to go into every new project with an open mind in order to get the most out of it and not have the work *tainted* by preconceived notions. I'm hopeful that your time with us here will be enlightening." She took a breath and put on her best smile. "That's about it for the tour, and I have a ton of work, as I'm sure you do as well. If you'll let Brenda know what you need for the public service announcement and when we can get started, I'd appreciate that." She stuck out her hand.

Reluctantly he took it. He was being dismissed. He would have laughed, but it wasn't funny.

"Thank you for stopping by." She ushered him toward the door of the main office. "Bren, Mr. Lawrence needs to give you some information." She flashed him a smile and had an instant of satisfaction from the stunned look on his face. "Have a good day." She turned and went downstairs.

For a moment he felt as if he'd been sent to sit in the corner. He could barely concentrate on what he needed to tell this woman in front of him for thinking about Dione and her ability to totally detach herself and make him feel two inches tall, and all with a dazzling smile.

"What day did you want to start?"

Garrett finally focused on Brenda's patient "he's slow" expression.

"At least by next week. You, or whoever is going to write it, need to write up a sixty-second script. Say whatever you think will get people to stand up and take notice."

He heard footsteps in the hall and turned his head toward the door, hoping it would be Dione. It wasn't.

Returning his attention to Brenda, he noticed she'd replaced her "he's slow" expression with "now you're getting on my nerves and I'm trying to be nice."

"I really think I should explain all of this to Ms. Williams. Especially since —"

She cut him right off. "Dione is very busy. I can assure you, Mr. Lawrence I'm quite capable of delivering the information. If she has any questions, she'll call you."

Just how many times would he get stung in one day? Did everyone in this place have the knack for putting you in deep check with the arch of a brow, or a turn of a phrase all done with a smile?

He gave her a grin with no teeth, then reached into his jacket pocket and pulled out a white business card. "Here's my card. My pager number is on there in case she can't reach me at the studio and my home number is on the back."

"I'll be sure she gets it." She gave the card a cursory glance and put it down on the desk. "Nice meeting you."

"You, too." But he wasn't really sure.

Brenda rose. "I'll walk you out."

When they reached the front door, Garrett stopped. "Is it always like this?" he asked, still a bit in awe, his eyes skipping once again over the interior, the smooth pale green walls adorned with inexpensive artwork and the shiny cream-colored linoleum floors.

"Like what?"

"Orderly. Clean. Quiet."

She chuckled. "We have our moments. Believe me. But for the most part everyone knows what's expected of them and what will and will not be tolerated. We do have rules, Mr. Lawrence."

He pressed his lips together and flicked his eyebrows. "Thanks again," he mumbled and stepped outside.

Dione paced the floor of her office like a caged tigress. It took all she had not to spew an earsplitting scream of frustration. She thought she'd gotten beyond allowing narrow-minded people to get to her. But Garrett Lawrence had sneaked in, passed the guard, and rattled her defenses.

She shouldn't let his prejudiced attitude affect her. But it had. Deeply. From the moment she'd set eyes on him she'd wanted him to be different. Not like all the others.

It was one of the many reasons why she'd avoided intimate relationships in general. Not that she was anticipating an intimate relationship with him, but whenever she met a man he either felt threatened by the time and devotion she gave to her work and the girls under her care, or believed that her talents could be better utilized in corporate America where she could make some *real* money.

They never understood that for her it was never about money, or about deciding who or what was more important — her work or them. For her it was about survival. And she had yet to meet a man whose passion for what he did came from a place deep inside of himself and the only way to get from one day to the next was to do what he truly believed in.

How could she trust him to honestly project the image of Chances Are if his opinions were so jaded?

She folded her arms beneath her breasts and halted her pacing. She needed this project to work. Chances Are needed this project. A smile of determination inched across her cinnamon-tinted lips.

Everyone who crossed the threshold of her domain slowly began to understand and even absorb the special essence that set it apart from all the rest. Hearts and minds had been changed within these very walls, under this roof. Garrett Lawrence would be a convert if it was the last thing she did.

On the drive back to the studio, Garrett kept thinking about his visit, not so much the shooting possibilities but the entire episode. Reality kept clashing with what he'd believed to be true. The constant butting of heads had thrown him completely off center.

He parked in front of the studio and went in, glad to see that Jason was still in the office. He tossed his battered leather flight jacket, followed by his cap on a vacant chair, then plopped down, stretching his legs out in front of him.

"So let's hear it. What's the place like?"

Garrett looked at Jason for a hot minute. The corner of his mouth flinched upward. "Believe me, it's nothing like I thought." He looked off toward the empty space, and a vision of Dione materialized before him. "Nothing at all," he whispered.

CHAPTER 7

The intercom on Dione's phone buzzed. She depressed the flashing red light.

"Yes, Brenda."

"Garrett Lawrence is on the phone."

Dione's eyebrows rose. He'd only been gone a little more than an hour. Had he changed his mind about working with them? "Thanks, Bren. I'll take it." She pressed the blinking yellow light. "Mr. Lawrence, I didn't expect to hear from you so soon. Is there a problem?"

"No. No problem. I, uh, I know I left some information with your assistant, but I felt it was better if I spoke to you directly. I hope I'm not disturbing you."

The message was clear enough, she thought, doing a quick mental replay of what Brenda had said, and couldn't imagine what was unclear.

"You're not disturbing me. I'm listening."

He cleared his throat, suddenly tongue-tied, knowing that the real reason why he called had nothing to do with the message he'd left.

"I was hoping that we could get together — before you come in to tape the PSA — go over a few things." He squeezed his eyes shut and hoped he didn't sound as idiotic as he felt.

Dione frowned. "Is that really necessary? I mean, I'm sure you can tell me what you need. I —"

"Why don't I just be honest," he cut in. "That's not the reason why I called." He blew out a breath through his teeth. "We — I started off on the wrong foot. And that's not the way to get into a business endeavor. I need to be objective and not bring my life or my opinions to the job. I was out of line with my comments."

"I hadn't noticed," she said fighting a smile.

"Well, I did, and I'm sorry."

"Consider your apology accepted."

For a moment no one spoke.

"Maybe we could meet tomorrow — after work. I'm done here about six," Dione said, not sure where that one had come from. But it was out now.

"Sounds good. You name the place."

"Have you ever been to Ashford and

Simpson's place, the Sugar Bar on —"

"Seventy-second," he chuckled, finishing her sentence.

"I take it you have. Hope that's a good thing."

"Definitely. Food's good. Great atmosphere. Say about seven — give you time to get there?"

"Seven is fine." She hesitated a moment. "So, I'll see you tomorrow."

"Looking forward to it."

Had his voice taken on a huskier note, or was she just imagining things?

"Tomorrow then."

"Have a good evening."

"You, too." Absently she hung up the phone. "Well, that conversation sure took a walk around the bend." She leaned back in her seat. "One minute I'm twisted out of shape because of his ugly attitude, and the next I'm meeting him for dinner. I must be losing my mind." She slapped her palms down on the desktop and stood, picking up several folders in the process.

"It must be the desperation in me," she mumbled, taking the folders to the gray metal file cabinet stuck in the corner of the room. She shoved the folders back in place and slammed the drawer shut, then stared at nothingness. "Or maybe it's the woman."

"Why are you sitting there with that silly grin on your face?" Jason asked, stepping into the office and setting a camera down on the table.

"I'm having dinner with Dione Williams tomorrow night."

Jason tossed his head back and laughed. "Gary man, you're a real piece of work. One minute I have to practically beg you kickin' and screamin' to take this job. The next you're having dinner with the client."

"Hey, what can I tell you. She — interests me and I think we got off to a bad start. I just want to set things straight."

"Over dinner? You could have done that over the phone."

"It was her suggestion."

"Hers?"

"Yeah. Why's that so hard to believe?"

Jason held up his hand. "It's your show, my brother. Just remember this is business. Don't let a pretty face and a great body screw up your head."

"Give me some credit, Jas. I know what I'm doing."

"Hmm. I'm gonna put this equipment back and then I'm out. See you tomorrow."

"Later."

Garrett sat at his desk for a good half hour, thinking about his visit to the shelter, his phone conversation with Dione and what Jason said.

He'd never made it a practice to get involved with his clients, but he was being pulled toward Dione. He wasn't sure what it was — her physical beauty, her quick wit or intelligence. Although they were certainly enticing pieces of the puzzle it was something deeper — the *thing* that made her tick. He wanted to know what that thing was. What drove her? What made a woman like Dione dedicate her life, her energy to a bunch of irresponsible girls?

He didn't think it was simply compassion, the ambiguous need to do good. No. It was something more than that. Just as he was driven to perfection, to striving for something more as if to compensate for his lack of a past, he constantly forged his own future, made things appear the way *he* wanted to see them. In that, he sensed they were the same — the drive, the need to surpass expectations. Perhaps he'd catch her shadows behind the cloak of his camera lens when she let down her guard and spoke from within. Everyone always did. Caught in the darkroom, staring into a camera lens was like looking into a mirror without a reflection. For the brief instant of unreality, when your gaze first connects and sinks into the apparent bottomlessness of the camera, the eyes tell it all.

He smiled. For the first time since he'd agreed to this job, he was actually looking forward to it. Maybe he'd even be able to show Dione just how futile it was to try to make something out of nothing. It was all just an illusion, and he should know; he'd become a master of making the unbelievable look believable.

"Don't second-guess yourself, Dee. I hear it in your voice," Terri said into the phone. "I told you I think it's a great idea," Terri said. "I could put together a dynamite presentation, once the PSA is done. What did this guy do to you to finally convince you to do this? I've been bugging you for months."

"I know. I guess I didn't want to admit how difficult things had really gotten. And for your information, he didn't *do* anything. I made the decision on my own." How could she explain what he did to her? She wasn't sure herself. Besides, she didn't want to sound like some airheaded teenager trying to explain this hot and fast fascination for some guy she'd just met.

Terri shifted the phone from her right side to her left, tucking it between her ear and shoulder as she polished her toenails.

"So — what's he like?"

"Your typical nonbeliever. But I just feel that his ambivalence stems from somewhere other than the usual prejudices about teen mothers."

"There goes the psychologist in you." Terri chuckled. "And you're on a crusade to change his mind."

Dione smiled. "Maybe."

"I think it's more than that."

"Why?"

"From all the things you're *not* saying. Remember, this is me. We've known each other since college, Dee. You haven't given a man the time of day in ages. Or cared what they thought."

"It's not like that."

"So what's it like?"

"It's just a business dinner, Terri. That's it."

"For now."

"Not funny."

"Hey, I'm not knocking you, girl. How many times have I said you need a life beyond your job and your daughter? Maybe something will come out of this — besides a public service announcement and a documentary."

"That's not what I'm looking for."

"You should be. Those girls are going to move on with their lives, just like the ones before them and those who come after. Niyah will be out on her own and you'll be alone. You deserve more than that."

"I have what I want. I worked for this. Struggled for it. All I'm concerned about right now is keeping Chances Are open. That's it."

"But getting a little somethin' out of it for yourself wouldn't hurt. I thought all I ever wanted was my career, until I met Clint. He makes everything I do worthwhile. He makes me feel complete."

Dione shook her head. "It's not that easy for me, Terri. You know that."

"You need to let it go. Every man is not your father."

Dione's insides twisted.

"You can't keep running away from men for the rest of your life — living vicariously through the girls and through Niyah."

"I'm not running. I'm where I want to be. I'm happy."

"Listen, girlfriend, who are you trying to convince, me or you? But, hey whatever you say. It's your life."

"Thanks. And on that note, I'm turning

in. It's getting late," she said needing to get off the phone and away from the truth.

"Are you going to talk to Niyah when she comes home for the holidays?"

Dione blew out a breath of indecision. "I don't know when, or if I will."

"Get some rest, Dee," Terri said, fighting to keep the frustration out of her voice. "Have a nice evening tomorrow."

"Thanks. Tell Clint I said hello."

"I will. Good night."

"Night."

Dione's dreams were tortured with images of that first night that she walked the streets, alone, terrified and cold with nowhere to go, no one she could turn to. She had her royal-blue backpack with her books and whatever else she could stuff in her bag, a shoulder bag with some toiletries and the envelope her mother had given her, and her one suitcase.

Walking along the darkened streets of Bedford-Stuyvesant, in the neighborhood that she lived in, played in, spent the best years of her life in, suddenly seemed sinister and unfriendly. The houses that she knew like the back of her hand were suddenly as unfamiliar as a foreign language.

She walked by her best friend Celeste's

house and for a moment, she stopped. Maybe Celeste's parents would let her stay with them? But if her father discovered that she'd found refuge, there was no telling what he might do. And she wouldn't go to Michael. She couldn't even tell him and ruin his chances for college.

She looked up to where she knew Celeste's bedroom window was, and her eyes clouded over. She kept walking. She couldn't involve her friends. She couldn't tell anyone. She was too ashamed. Ashamed at what she'd done. Ashamed for what her parents had done to her. How could she tell her friends, tell anyone that she was homeless? A bum. That her family didn't want her.

To this day, nearly two decades later, the pain was just as fresh as if it had been inflicted only moments ago.

Yes, she'd made a life for herself, maybe trying to prove something to herself and to the world, that she wasn't just another statistic. But deep in her soul she knew that Terri was right. She was hiding behind her work and her daughter. Only now, after all this time, she didn't know how to step out from behind the walls, as much as she may have wanted to. It was her haven. Someplace where she and her feelings were safe.

She turned on her side and a vision of her

daughter took the place of the doorway she'd slept in that first night.

Niyah stood there, tears streaming down her face.

"How could you have lied to me? All these years. You lied. I believed in you. Trusted you. But you never felt the same way about me. I hate you! You hear me — hate you!"

Dione's eyes flew open. Her heart raced.

She couldn't risk that. No. She wouldn't risk Niyah ever finding out the truth. She didn't know what she'd do if she ever lost her precious daughter's love.

She pressed her hands to her stomach, hoping to calm the swirling sensation. She knew what she'd have to do and she hated herself for it. But she had no other choice.

All anyone ever had to know was what she told them.

CHAPTER 8

When morning came, Dione was tense and groggy from her nightmare-filled sleep. Her eyes were puffy and red-rimmed and her body was sluggish like a clogged drain. She moved through the apartment in slow motion trying to get her rhythm going.

Since she wouldn't have time to go home and change before her meeting with Garrett, she took extra special care with her choice of clothing, and to hide the circles under her eyes, she even wore a hint of makeup, something she rarely did.

Standing in front of the full-length mirror, that was attached behind her bedroom door, she assessed the impression she would make. Not too business, but not too casual, she concluded turning from side to side, the magenta coatdress projected just the right impression.

She sighed, wondering again why it was so important what Garrett Lawrence thought. She sipped her coffee, the second cup of the morning. This meeting was about coming to some common goals and hopefully steering his way of thinking into a more positive direction. But about what, she asked herself. Her, or Chances Are?

For years she'd been plagued by what others thought of her. About who and what she was. It had become exceedingly important that she represent what could be achieved.

And she had achieved. She had shattered the stereotypes, but at what cost? There was still a part of her that refused to acknowledge the ugly truth of her life. The isolation and loss she felt. As a result, she'd become an overachiever, hoping somehow to fill the voids in her soul with external successes.

She turned away from the telling reflection. This wasn't about her. It was about saving her business, saving those girls who had no one else. And as she always had done, she tucked her personal feelings into that dark corner of her heart where they couldn't be reached.

"Mmm. Don't you look jazzy today. A little tired, but jazzy," Brenda commented when Dione arrived at work. "Love that dress."

"Thanks." Dione hung up her coat.

"Special occasion?" she hedged.

"I'm having a business dinner with Mr. Lawrence this evening — to iron out some details," she added, catching the arched eyebrow expression.

"I'm sure he'll be impressed."

Dione flashed her a look. "It's business, Bren. That's it."

"Fine. Don't get bent out of shape. But he is a good-looking brother. I know I wouldn't mind sitting across a table from him." She turned to her computer and began typing.

Dione hesitated a moment, debating whether to open up the subject, then decided; why not?

"Brenda?"

"Hmm?"

"What are your impressions of him?"

Brenda swiveled in her chair in Dione's direction. "Honestly?"

"Of course."

"Well —" She blew out a breath. "Besides being drop-dead fine, I think he has a chip on his shoulder and some serious issues about teen mothers. My only concern is how that is going to affect his slant on our program."

Dione nodded. "I have the same feeling," she replied thoughtfully.

"Hey, if anybody can convert him, you can."

"That remains to be seen. But it's definitely my intention."

"I was going to hold this tidbit of information, but you may as well know. I got a call this morning from the Slattery Foundation."

Dione could tell she didn't want to hear what Brenda had to say. "Tell me why they don't want to give us any funding," she said already resigned to the outcome.

"The contribution's chairwoman said that the Foundation wants to move away from programs that intentionally or inadvertently support dependency."

"Support dependency! How can they say that? Our entire goal is to get these girls self-sufficient so they *won't* be dependent on a system that's set up for them to fail. Brenda the narrow-mindedness just turns my stomach." Her face twisted in anger.

"I know. I felt like jumping through the phone and smacking some sense into her."

Dione could have laughed if she wasn't so angry. She could just about see Brenda doing something like that. "I guess this is even more reason to make this thing work."

"For sure."

Dione ran her fingers through her hair, which she'd decided to wear down today instead of in her standard ponytail. "I'll be downstairs. Any other developments I need to know about before I bury myself in paperwork?"

Brenda pulled out the sheet from the previous night's activities that Betsy completed. "Nothing major. Gina's baby was running a slight fever. She's taking her to the doctor today. I think she's teething, personally. Umm, Theresa set off the smoke detector again. One of these days that girl is going to figure out that the smoke detector is not a food timer." They both laughed. "Denise lost her front door key. I'll see about having it replaced. That's about it."

"Okay. Just hold off on replacing Denise's key. This is the second one she's lost in less than a month."

"Will do," Brenda said, amazed at the tiny details that Dione always remembered no matter how many really important things she had to deal with.

"I'll be downstairs."

Dione spent the better part of the morning reviewing the pit Chances Are was sinking into. She felt like the unfortunate captain of the *Titanic*. Disaster everywhere, help on the horizon but not close enough. Abandon ship, or wait to be rescued?

She turned on her computer and pulled up the database of funders, seeing whom she may have missed, knowing she hadn't missed anyone.

There had to be a better way, she mused. The hoops that organizations had to go through to receive funding in order to survive, in order to provide basic human services was sadistic. Yet the government wouldn't bat an eye to pay thousands of dollars for a toilet seat, or a screw. There was something obscene about that.

She stared at the list of names and addresses projected against the screen. Christmas was less than three months away. A difficult time for all of them because of their situations. She always tried to make the holidays extra special for the girls and their kids because of that. The last thing she wanted to have to do was tell them they had to start making preparations to leave.

Her intercom buzzed.

"Yes, Bren?"

"It's Mr. Lawrence for you," she said in a ha, ha tone.

Dione frowned. "Thanks." She pressed the yellow button. "Mr. Lawrence."

"Hi. I'm sure you're busy, but I'm hoping you're not."

She laughed. "Really. Why is that?"

"It just so happens that I'm free for the rest of the afternoon and I was hoping I could tear you away from what you were doing. You could come by the studio — work out the details of the PSA and then we could go to dinner."

Her eyes widened. This was beginning to sound more like a date than a business meeting by the minute. Did she really want that? What would they have to talk about?

What in the world was he doing? He wasn't quite sure where the idea had come from. He'd been thinking about her all morning and anticipating seeing her later. That much he knew. Then all of a sudden he was dialing her number and asking her to cut her day short and spend the time with him. Now listening to the nothingness that separated them, he was beginning to feel like a real dope. And what must she be thinking?

"Sounds great. I need to get out of here. Maybe a change of environment would be just the thing I need." *There, she'd said it. She'd stuck her big toe across the invisible line.*

The cobra-like grip that had wrapped around his insides from the moment he'd put his finger on the telephone buttons, seemed to begin to unwind, release him, letting him take a deep breath.

"Whenever you're ready, I'll be here." *Did he sound like he was grinning?*

"I'll see you in about an hour."

"See you then." Slowly he hung up the phone and immediately wondered what he'd done.

Dione stared at the phone, her stomach doing tiny somersaults. *You know good and well that you have enough work to keep you busy until after the new year.* And the last thing she needed to do was spend any unnecessary time with Garrett Lawrence. What she needed to use now was her head, not relying on the suddenness of emotions that he'd somehow stirred up inside her, which seemed to be leading her down a path she spent most of her time avoiding.

Garrett Lawrence was not different from the rest. She'd already seen as much. But there was that something else she'd seen as well. Something that he kept buried beneath his attitude, leather jacket and baseball cap. That was the flame that drew her.

She didn't want to get burned.

For a moment she shut her eyes, then she opened her desk drawer, took out her purse and went upstairs.

"I'm going to be out of the office for the rest of the afternoon, Brenda," Dione said reaching for her coat. "I'll call in for messages."

Brenda watched Dione do anything she could not to look her right in the eye. "Everything okay?"

"Yes. I'm going to the studio — and then from there, dinner." Oh, God she felt so silly. It was infantile to feel this truckload of guilt. But she'd felt that way for years. Guilty for ever wanting anything for herself. Even if it was just sometimes.

"Enjoy yourself."

Dione looked at Brenda who gave her a soft smile of encouragement.

"Thanks. Page me if you need me."

"Let's hope I don't. I'm sure we can handle whatever comes up."

"Okay, then. But you know you can if you have to. See you in the morning." Dione slipped on her coat and turned to leave.

"Dee —"

"Hmm?"

"Forget about this place. At least for a little while."

Dione gave a half smile and walked out.

On the entire twenty-minute drive over to the studio, Dione vacillated between heading back, and meeting Garrett as planned. A premonition, as certain as the ache in Betsy's knees when rain was coming, had settled in her center. This meeting was the start of something. She knew it as sure as she knew her name.

But she had to stay focused. She had an agenda, and that was to get beyond Garrett's stereotypical mentality so that the project would be a success. That was it, first and foremost. She couldn't be dissuaded by dimpled smiles, manly scents, a crooning voice and husky laughter.

A shiver ran through her when the sudden recollection of his warm breath had caressed her neck and his fingertips had brushed her shoulders.

A horn blared behind her. She looked up and realized she'd been sitting at a green light. Shaking her head she pulled out across the intersection. *This was not good.*

"Hot coals under your feet or something, brother?" Jason asked from across the studio floor as he adjusted one of the three cameras.

Garrett halted his pacing and looked at his friend. *Busted.* "Can't a man walk and think in this place or what?"

Jason's mouth twisted in a grin. "Must be heavy. You've been burning a hole in the floor for the past ten minutes."

Garrett stuck his hands in his pockets and

blew out a breath. How could he explain what was going on inside of him? Although he and Jason were tight, and had been for a while, Jason didn't know everything. Not about his beginnings, the kind of life he'd led and why. He'd never been able to share that with anyone. Jason just thought of him as the consummate playboy, "the man," with a three-hundred-and-sixty-five day assortment of women. None of whom mattered to him beyond the moment.

But as quick as a pop of your fingers to the beat, Dione had crept under his skin. Although her very existence, what she represented smacked him square in the face with his own reality, she also awakened the human side of him that had been dormant for longer than he could remember.

"This may sound . . . strange, but this meeting, dinner thing with Dione has me kind of on edge." He sneaked a peek at Jason to see his reaction.

"It happens to all of us, man. Even you." He looked across the room at Garrett. "There's always that one woman who makes you kind of crazy for no apparent reason. Maybe she's the one. You can't analyze it like a storyboard for a television script. You'll make yourself nuts. Just go with it."

"Is that how it happened with you and

Tricia?"

Jason let out a short laugh. "It was more like getting hit over the head with a brick. First time I saw her, I knew it was over for me." He shook his head. "Still don't understand it."

Garrett smiled. Even though Jason talked a good game with women, Garrett knew Jason was devoted to his wife of five years. It had never been like that when he married Gayle. His reasons had nothing to do with stars exploding in front of his eyes. It had more to do with hoping he could find something he'd been looking for all his life, someone to care about him. His problem had been he didn't know how to care back. And as much as he was beginning to think he wanted to see where things could go with Dione, he still didn't know if he was capable of returning to her or to anyone, the one thing that he needed himself: love."

"I guess I better look out for falling bricks."

"No doubt, brother."

Dione pulled up in front of the studio and sat in her car for a good five minutes, trying to play out all the scenarios for the rest of the evening. Maybe after the studio meeting she could feign a headache and take a raincheck on dinner. Maybe she should use her cell phone and call, tell him she had an emergency at the house and couldn't get away. Maybe she should act like a grown woman, get out of the car and go out with the man. What was the worst thing that could happen: she'd find out he was a real bastard and that would end any fantasies she may have been conjuring up about anything beyond this project. But she'd never know if she never got out of the car.

Checking her reflection in the rearview mirror, she opened the door and stepped out. She took in a lungful of air.

It's showtime.

CHAPTER 9

Garrett's body jerked when the buzz from the front door shot through him like a bolt of lightning. He pushed away from the edit board and took a quick look at his watch. It had been forty-five minutes since he'd spoken with Dione. It must be her. But he didn't want to act as anxious as he felt. He'd just play it cool until somebody came to get him.

His thumping heartbeat counted out the seconds. It seemed like forever. Maybe it wasn't even her. But then again, she was probably being given the third degree by the part-time secretary and his personal nemesis, Marva English, who felt it her duty to make people as uncomfortable as possible, especially women who came to see him. If she wasn't so incredibly good at what she did, he would have fired her a long time ago. But Marva ran G.L. Productions with a precision that was almost frightening. Her attention to detail and keeping the business on top of their expenses was almost worth the torture of having her there.

Jason always said Marva's biggest and only problem was that she wanted Garrett for herself and resented any woman whom she viewed as a potential threat to her master plan. Garrett, of course, thought the entire idea was ridiculous.

It wasn't that Marva was outright rude. She just had the uncanny knack of making you feel as if you'd been put under the interrogation lights.

Thinking about it, he jumped up out of his seat with the intention of rescuing Dione when there was a short knock on the door. He saw Marva's pale, butter-toned face and intricately braided strawberry blond head through the rectangular glass in the door.

Before he could do the honors, Marva let herself in. Her expression was pinched, her cheeks flushed — from makeup or aggravation he couldn't tell.

"There's a woman here to see you. A Ms. Williams. She doesn't have an appointment," she almost sneered, emphasizing *doesn't.* "But she said you were expecting her."

"I am. And thank you. Ms. Williams is a

new client. She's the head of the residence we'll be doing the documentary on."

Her expression slowly cleared. The crease between her brown eyes eased. "Oh. It would help a lot, Gary, if you'd let me know these things so that I can put the appointment in the book and be prepared."

He gave her a replica of a smile. "My fault. I apologize. This was last minute."

"Well, she's in the waiting room."

"Thanks, Marva."

"I'll let her know you'll be right with her." She closed the door and Garrett raised his eyes to the ceiling. *Who was really running this place, anyway?*

He pulled the door open and walked out into the adjoining space that served as their waiting area.

For a hot minute he stood in the open archway watching her, the dazzling pink outfit reminding him of the early embers of a raging flame. Although she appeared reserved, almost aloof with her long legs crossed, her shoulders erect while scanning a magazine, he sensed that there was definitely fire beneath her ultracool, very conservative exterior.

Dione felt his presence and slowly turned her head in his direction. When their gazes connected, and his smile touched down on her, she felt her insides shift, then slowly settle.

"Hi." In three long strides he was standing above her. "Glad you could come." His gaze rolled over her face. "Let's talk in the back."

She replaced the magazine on the black, circular table and stood. "Very pleasant secretary you have," she commented, the subtle sarcasm not wasted on Garrett.

He laughed lightly, placing his hand on the small of her back as he ushered her along, and it took all she had to contain the sudden shudder that rushed up her spine. "She's actually quite harmless," he said in hushed tones. "She has so many other special qualities that we treasure."

She looked at him over her shoulder to see if he was kidding. She couldn't tell from the sparkle in his eyes and didn't want to speculate on what her "special qualities" were. All she did know was that Marva whoever, couldn't work for her for five minutes. There was no room for abrasiveness and short dispositions at her domain. Her staff was constantly reminded to leave their bad nights and poor attitudes at the door. To each his own. But, once again the question of integrity resurfaced.

"I was in the editing suite. I thought we

could talk there while I finished up a short video."

He held the door open for her and caught the soft scent of her as she brushed by him and entered the dimly lit space.

"Why do you work with the lights almost out?" she immediately asked, a bit unsettled by the intimate atmosphere. She took a seat farthest away from the control board.

"It's easier to see the images on the screen and the lighted dials with the lights down." He looked at her from the corner of his eye. "What did you think the reason was?"

She couldn't very well tell him that she thought it was because he was trying to get cozy and only did it when she was around. That obviously wasn't the case. "I wasn't sure." She examined the heel of her shoe.

"Want to slide over here and see what I'm doing? It's similar to what you want done."

Sit right next to him? "Sure." She took the vacant seat in front of the board.

"What I'm doing," he began, "is viewing the raw footage that was taken at the company's location and here in the studio. Then I can determine what pieces I want to use and the editing process begins."

"The client doesn't have any input on what gets cut and what doesn't?"

"That's why we have a meeting before I

shoot. Most of my clients are repeats. They trust me." He looked into her eyes, then quickly looked away. "They tell me what they want and I make it happen." He shrugged. "Then there are those clients who want to be in on every square inch of production. Drives me crazy. I generally avoid working with them again."

Was that a hint? She'd like to think that she could leave it to his discretion to project the best image of Chances Are. But chances were, he wouldn't. "Hmm," was all she said.

"Here, slide a little closer. I'll let you work on it with me."

She shook her head, smiling nervously. "No, I —"

"Of course you can." He took her hands and placed them on what looked like a keyboard. "Do you type?"

"Yes."

"Great. I don't. Just type what I tell you on the character generator and it will appear on the monitor."

"Are you sure about this?"

"That you can type, or that's what the machine really does?"

She grinned. "None of the above. Are you sure you want *me* to do this?"

"Sure. Why not? You're here. I'm here." He swallowed before he really blurted out something ridiculous. "This will make good use of our time and actually help me out in the process."

"Okay. Fire away."

As she typed the list of names and titles for the credits, he gently and patiently explained how to correct errors, what some of the titles for the crew meant, and shortcuts to get the machine to repeat the previous action without having to retype the information. She was actually enjoying herself and quickly got the hang of working the machine.

She was keenly aware of his presence, his maleness, when he leaned close to help her, the bottomless pitch of his voice when he explained something, the soulfulness of his laughter, the power yet slenderness of his fingers as he manipulated controls. But instead of it making her uncomfortable as she'd anticipated, she welcomed it, allowed it to flow through and around her without analyzing it.

Her years of training in psychology and in social work had taught her to be analytical, rational, to dissect the information in front of her and come up with a solution. As a result she constantly wanted to deal with what could either be explained by a medical term or solved with some sort of case management plan. There was nothing in her textbooks or in the endless lectures and seminars that taught her how to keep her emotions at bay. Like now. With Garrett. Like all the times she cried herself to sleep when she couldn't help one of the girls. So her rational mind and her giving, needy heart were in constant conflict.

Almost too soon they were finished.

Garrett leaned back in his seat, stretched and talked, his voice coming out like one long satisfied yawn. "All done. Thanks. It would have taken me at least another hour if I had to type it myself."

"I find that hard to believe," she said, after having watched the nimbleness of his fingers.

"Trust me. I turn into all thumbs. Give me a camera and an edit board and you can't get any better. I can make magic happen." He turned to her and flashed that grin.

She wanted to ask him if that's all he was good at. It was right on the tip of her tongue and she snatched it back. Quick.

He switched on the lights and she suddenly felt off balance as if she'd been jerked awake from a peaceful sleep.

"I did want to show you the raw footage of the PSA we did." He leaned over at a precarious angle to reach for a tape stacked on the floor next to his chair.

Agile, too.

"Here we go." He straightened himself back up. "What you saw the other day was more or less the finished product." He pushed the oversized tape in the deck opening, pressed several buttons, and dimmed the lights, again.

As she watched the montage of scenes and obvious retakes, she was amazed at what the end result had actually been.

"How long did it take you to tape all of this?"

"About three days." He pointed to the monitor as he spoke. "Most people are used to seeing a talking head do these things." He caught her confused frown. "In other words, no interaction, no real background, just someone sitting in a chair telling you how wonderful they are or their company is." He shook his head. "Real boring stuff. My goal is to create something memorable every time I get behind the camera lens."

He turned to her and the intensity in his eyes shook her to her core, and she found herself holding her breath.

"Have you thought about what you wanted to say — the points you want to get across?"

She cleared her throat releasing the knot

of air. "Not in detail, but I have a general idea. I like the idea of it being more than just me staring into a camera talking."

"We can do whatever you want." He smiled. "I'll handle everything else. And I know you'll be pleased with the outcome."

"I'm sure I will."

For a moment, they simply stared at one another, each walking along the road of words unsaid.

He knew he'd been rattling, tooting his own horn. It was suddenly important to him that she felt good about him, about them working together. Most times it didn't matter one way or the other what a client thought about him personally. It was just a job. But Dione was different. He felt as if he had something to prove. And he wasn't quite sure why. She was the first woman he'd met in a while that intrigued him both physically and mentally. Dione was a woman standing on her own two feet, running her own business. These days it took guts, instinct and plenty of determination to run and operate a successful business, especially in New York. He knew first-hand and had to give her her due, whether he agreed with the root of what she did or not.

She probably should give him one of the excuses she'd devised while she'd sat in her car, she thought, make her escape while she could. But the truth was, she didn't want to. As much as she was reluctant to admit it, she wanted to be in his company, listen to him talk, see his smile, hear his laughter. And the realization unnerved her. It had been far too long since she'd opened herself to the possibility of "maybe." And looking at his eyes and soft, encouraging smile, she couldn't quite remember what those excuses were.

"Ready?" he asked, breaking into her thoughts.

She nodded.

"Great." He stood up. "Let me tell Marva I'm leaving."

Dione got up as well and followed him out.

"I'll be gone for the rest of the day," he told Marva, who instantly gave Dione the once over.

"I see," she said, but didn't sound as if she did. "Is there somewhere you can be reached in case of an emergency?"

Garrett peered at her for a moment as if he'd lost his seeing glasses. "I can't imagine what emergency there would be that can't be handled without me."

"Anything could happen," she said, a

slight edge to her tone.

Garrett blew out an exasperated breath. "Jason should be back shortly. And I'll be back in the morning. Have a good evening." He turned to Dione, placed his hand on the small of her back, and ushered her out.

"Is she always like that?" Dione asked under her breath, as they walked down the corridor, wondering if there was something more than just employer-employee going on between them.

"Most of the time," he muttered. "Sometimes she's worse."

Dione shook her head, mystified. "I don't want to get into your business, or how you run it but if that's how she is and sometimes worse, why do you tolerate it?"

"I've probably asked myself that question at least a million times. But barring her less than cordial attitude, Marva is the best secretary-office manager I've ever worked with. She's phenomenal with numbers, keeps our books in tip top shape and pays all the bills on time. She's unbelievable when it comes to details that Jason and I invariably forget. She doesn't miss a trick. I think she's just become very possessive of all of us." He shrugged. "I live with it."

He opened the door and held it for her.

When they got outside, Garrett walked

toward the direction of his car and Dione walked toward hers. They both stopped halfway, looked at each other and laughed.

Typical, she thought, needing to add fuel to the "I don't want to like him" fire. *He just took it for granted that I didn't drive.*

"Should we take separate cars, or would you like to ride with me?"

I should have bet money. But beside his arrogant assumption, the thought of sitting so close to him in such a confined space going and coming set her nerves on edge. She wasn't quite ready for that.

"Then you'd have to bring me all the way back to pick my car up. It would be easier if I took mine. After all it's *not* a date."

"I agree. Whatever you say. But it's still no problem for me to bring you back, date or not." He knew what she said made plenty of sense but he still hoped. "Really."

The offer was tempting. . . . She gave a short shake of her head. "No. I'd rather take my car."

"All right." He opened his driver's side door. "I'm taking F.D.R. Drive. Do you know how to get there if we get separated?"

"No problem."

"See you there, then." He slid behind the wheel, shut the door and turned on the engine, then revved it a few times.

Hope he's not one of those daredevil drivers, she thought, getting into her car and pulling out behind him, even though she knew she could keep up with the best of them. One of her few passions was long-distance driving — fast. She smiled. Maybe she'd make him follow her.

Which is exactly what he had to do. Dione made it a point of darting in and out of traffic, zooming through yellow lights and staying in the fast lane once they reached the highway.

Periodically, she checked her rearview mirror and every time Garrett got close, she'd dart around a car in front of her, or switch lanes. She didn't know about him, but she was having a ball.

While Garrett kept her in his eyesight, he began to get the distinct impression that Dione wasn't so much in a hurry to get where they were going, but to take a little wind out of his sail. He may have been in control at the studio, but she was making her statement on the road. It was a good thing he knew where he was going.

By the time they arrived in front of the Sugar Bar, Dione felt exhilarated, even though there wasn't anywhere to park.

Garrett pulled up alongside her car and rolled down his window. Dione lowered hers and leaned toward the passenger door.

"There's a garage on the next block."

"Lead the way," she said with a grin, and Garrett wondered if she was trying to be funny. He pulled out and headed for the garage.

It had been a while since she'd been at Nick Ashford's and Valerie Simpson's restaurant, but it was just as cozy as the last time she'd visited.

The walls were adorned with African masks, and straw accessories that gave the impression of mounted huts on the cream-colored walls, and though the space was small, there was just enough room between the white linen-topped tables to allow for privacy.

But she couldn't have been more thrilled than to see Valerie Simpson sitting at the bar with her husband, Nick, both in conversation with a customer.

"Hi, Val. Long time," Dione greeted when Valerie turned in her direction. They gave each other a long-time-no-see hug and Nick kissed her cheek. Dione made the introductions and Nick insisted that drinks were on the house for old times' sake.

Garrett worked real hard to be cool and not have his mouth hang open after having been introduced to two of the music industry's superstars. But what really had him stunned was the very idea that Dione knew them — apparently very well.

They were seated at a cozy table in the corner, the only thing separating them were their knees, which almost touched, and the white candle that flicked in the glass bowl.

Garrett pretended to look at his menu, but he couldn't concentrate on what was in front of him. He peeked at Dione over the top of the menu and she looked as cool and in control as she always did, as if hanging with celebrities was an everyday occurrence.

There was no way he could hold his curiosity in check a minute longer. He put the menu down.

"How do you know them?"

"Who?" she asked, coyly.

He twisted his mouth. "You have a strange sense of humor, Ms. Williams. First it's the chase through Manhattan, then gripping and grinning with celebrities."

Dione giggled. "You didn't enjoy the ride?"

"Very funny." He looked at her seeing yet a new side of Dione, the playful, teasing side. He liked it.

Leaning forward, he braced his arms on the table. "Fine. Don't tell me. It can be your little secret. But," he shook his finger at her, "one of these days there's going to be something you're going to want me to tell you." He picked up his water glass and took a sip.

Dione bit back a smile. "What might you know that I'd want to find out, Mr. Lawrence — one of these days?"

"That remains to be seen. But I can guarantee it will be something."

She liked the way his eyes had suddenly darkened and his lowered voice reached down into her insides and gently stroked them.

"I'll keep that in mind." She picked her menu back up as the waiter approached. She ordered the spiced African shrimp and Garrett ordered the grilled salmon.

"So — what made you get into the video business?" Dione asked while they waited.

He gave a slight shrug. He couldn't very well tell her that it was his way of escape from the realities of his life. His one way of creating things the way he wanted them to be. That when he was behind the camera or closeted in the editing suite it was when he felt in control. She didn't need to know that.

"I guess I have a creative streak. I like what I can do with what I imagine. After bouncing from one corporate job to another, I got involved when a small video company came to one of my former places of employment to film a training video. I got to talking with some member of the crew and the rest is G.L. Productions." At least that part was true.

Dione watched him as he talked, the way his eyes didn't quite meet hers, the subtle but telltale lack of conviction in his voice. She'd listened to enough tales from the girls who crossed her doorstep. The way they were able to intricately weave a story to hide their hurt, their shame, their fears. They had that same look in their eyes as Garrett had now. And she was a classic case with her own version of her own reality.

What was it that Garrett hid behind the camera lens and the dimly lit room?

"What about you? I just don't see you — managing a shelter."

She felt her heart pinch and her stomach flutter. The positive feelings she'd begun to build about Garrett began to fizzle out like a soda gone flat.

"Who *do* you see managing a shelter?"

He'd done it again. He hadn't meant to, but it just slipped out. But it was the truth. "I didn't mean it like that."

"What did you mean? No. Don't answer that. Why don't we start from the core of what's bothering you?"

"And that is?"

"Your animosity toward teen mothers for starters."

His thoughts spun backward to the group homes, the foster families, the loneliness and feelings of not belonging, not being good enough to be cared about, all because of a girl who thought she was a woman and found out too late that she wasn't — at his expense.

He looked down at his hands, his fingers splayed on the tabletop. "It's just that what they've done to themselves, to their children is totally irresponsible and —" He shook his head. "The children suffer as a result. Families suffer and society is made to carry the burden with welfare."

"People make mistakes, and deserve every opportunity to correct them," she said her voice taking on a faraway note. "There was a time when young girls in trouble had nowhere to go. They found themselves shut off from their families, with nothing ahead of them but poverty and a long, dismal future. Many weren't up to the challenge."

His mother.

"Chances Are isn't about making life easy. It's about giving those girls and their children a chance to be contributors to society, not a burden."

If he didn't know better he'd think she was talking about herself. But that was crazy. *Dione? Impossible.*

"Maybe in the long run, but in the meantime doesn't providing all the creature comforts give other girls the idea that 'making a mistake' is all right?"

She took a sip of her water. "How many stories have you heard about young girls leaving their babies in alleys, in bathrooms, in garbage cans?"

A spot in his stomach started to burn, ignited by the memories of his own beginnings.

"Those are just a portion of them who felt so frightened and hopeless, that was their only choice. My goal is to keep that from happening to as many young girls as possible. And yes, in the meantime there will be those who think they're getting a free ride. But I'd rather that than read about them in the paper. Kids are being tried and put away for murder because they were either afraid to go to their parents for help, or felt they had no choices. Their lives were over because that's what we're told by society — a young girl has a baby and her life is over. Fear is a very powerful emotion."

Their food arrived and Dione focused all of her attention on the giant shrimp on her plate. She knew this was a mistake. She should have followed her first thought and canceled. She stabbed a shrimp with her fork. How could anyone, seemingly without effort, awaken emotions in her that she'd kept at bay, and in the next breath prove himself to be the king of bigotry, a narrow-minded fool that set her teeth on edge? She stabbed another shrimp.

She wishes that was me on that plate, he thought, cringing inside each time she attacked a shrimp.

What she'd said hit him where he lived. Maybe she was right. A part of him knew she was, but he wasn't quite ready to let go of his anger. He'd held on to it too long.

He put a slice of salmon in his mouth, chewing thoughtfully. Would his life have been different if his mother had had somewhere to turn all those years ago?

"What you do," he began with hesitation, "it's hard for me to accept."

Her gaze slowly rose and rested on his face. The bravado was gone. The challenge in his eyes and in his voice was gone. Replaced by what appeared to be regret. But not so much regret for what he'd said, regret for something much deeper.

128

Instinctively she reached out and clasped his fisted left hand. "We all have our demons to battle, Mr. Lawrence. In our own way. I've come to accept that in people. All I can do, all any of us can do is put up a good fight."

She smiled softly and Garrett felt as if she'd opened the window to his soul, took a peek inside and wasn't afraid of what she saw.

"Is that what you do every day, Ms. Williams, put up a good fight?"

"I give it my best. Just like you."

He wanted to uncoil his fist, take her hand, hold it, and bring it to his lips. It was just that kind of moment. But he knew better. As if reading his thoughts, she took her hand away.

He gave her a half smile. "It seems as if we may have crossed one of the great divides. I think that constitutes the use of first names. My friends call me Gary."

Dione lowered her gaze a moment, her heart beating a bit too fast, then looked up. "Mine call me Dee."

"Friends?"

"Friends."

They spent the balance of the meal sharing stories about their careers, her early days in real estate and his in video. Garrett had her choking on her wine spritzer with a story about a crazy request he'd gotten from a ninety-year-old client who ambled into his office about three weeks into operation and asked for an X-rated video of him and his thirty-year-old wife. And the array of clients who, no matter how hard you tried, were never satisfied, even though you'd done exactly what they asked. "The problem is, they don't know what they want to begin with," he said.

"And of course that's your fault," she said laughing.

"Of course."

Dione shared some of the high points of her time at Chances Are. The success stories and some of the failures. "But I enjoy the holidays most. It's a beautiful thing to see the girls and their children gather around our tree. For most of them we're the only family they have. Some of them visit with friends, or distant relatives but most of them don't. So the staff works extra hard to make it special."

Moment by moment he was beginning to see Chances Are through Dione's eyes, through her enthusiasm. Everyone had a calling. That was hers and he couldn't help but admire what she was doing, even if he couldn't quite come to grips with the reasons why she had to in the first place.

"Can I ask you something?"

She gave him a raised eyebrow look. "Okay. Ask."

He leaned forward a bit. "Why did you finally agree to the documentary?"

She took a breath and weighed her response. She could simply say she just decided it was a good idea, or she could tell him the truth. She paused for a long moment.

"Chances Are is in serious financial trouble," she finally admitted. "If we don't get funding in the next four to six months we'll have to close and those girls and their children will be placed in city shelters, or worse. Many of them won't want to go and without family to turn to they'll wind up on the street." Her heart thumped. Every time she thought about it, not to mention say it out loud, she had a momentary panic attack as she watched herself wander the streets at night, sleeping in filthy shelters and on train cars.

Garrett frowned. "What?"

She blinked away the vision then slowly nodded. "We wanted to use the documentary as both a promotional tool and a demonstration to potential funders as to

131

what we're really about and the need for us to stay in existence. But when you said it would take that long to finish it, I thought maybe the PSA would help a little in the meantime. My friend Terri Powers —"

"The public relations diva?"

She smiled. "You've heard of her, I take it?"

"Who hasn't? She handles some big-time accounts. *She's* a friend of yours, too?"

Dione laughed outright at that one. "Yes. Terri and I go back quite a few years."

The question was on the tip of his tongue: if you have all these high-powered friends, why is your business in trouble? And in the next breath he realized why. Dione Williams was a proud woman. Not one to run to friends for favors, or ask for help. She wanted to handle her own affairs, even if she had to struggle in the process.

"So what is your friend Terri planning to do?"

"I'm going to put the tape in her hands and let her work her magic."

He nodded. This certainly put a new twist on things, and on his perspective. The situation must have been pretty desperate for Dione to go against all her policies and instincts to agree to this project. The very idea that a project he worked on had the potential to save an organization, and more importantly a very special individual, gave him that last shot of inspiration that he needed. The finished product would be the best thing he'd done. Grant or no grant.

"I want to get started on the PSA before the end of the week," he said turning intense and serious.

Dione had to adjust her train of thought to catch up with the sudden change in Garrett. But she liked it. She liked the fire in his eyes and the way he could shift from stand-up comedian to introspective to the cynic to the serious man about business. What other hidden personas hovered beneath the surface of this obviously complex man?

"Do you think you could work out what you'd need to say by the end of the day tomorrow?"

"I — think so. Sure."

"Good. I'd like to come back to your office, get some footage to use along with your audio. I know it'll be more effective than just to have you in the studio talking into a camera. Although I'm sure you'll be wonderful," he added, reverting to the charmer.

Suddenly she felt vulnerable, exposed under the heat of his stare. She looked away, focusing on the remainder of her food.

Garrett Lawrence was a very interesting man.

"Thank you for a great dinner," she said, as they stood side by side in the garage waiting for their cars to be brought down from the upper level, and pretending they weren't inhaling the exhaust fumes that hung in the air like storm clouds.

"I enjoyed it and the company."

She glanced at him, feeling his stare. Her heart knocked against her chest. How was she going to maintain a professional relationship with this man if she turned into a ball of nerves every time he looked at her?

She's beautiful, he thought, *inside and out.* This was the first woman in ages who had him thinking about more than just the moment — maybe tomorrow.

He took a quiet breath and looked away. Dione hadn't given him the slightest indication that she was interested in anything more than the services he could provide. So there was no point in speculating.

Dione's car was brought down first, followed shortly after by Garrett's. She walked over to her car and dug in her purse to tip the driver when she felt a hand halt her action. She looked up at Garrett.

"I'll take care of it. Tonight is my treat."

She'd insisted from the start of the evening that this "wasn't a date" and he'd heartily agreed, but wouldn't give in. They'd had a brief debate at the restaurant about the bill until she finally gave in and let him pay. No sense in challenging the program now, she mused. *It was a guy thing.*

He followed the driver to the cashier's booth.

While he took care of the bill and the tip, she got in her car and buckled up. By the time he returned, she was revved up and ready to go, relieved to breathe the recycled air in her car.

He stopped alongside her door, and she rolled down her window.

"Do you want me to follow you home, make sure you arrive safely?"

There was that smile again.

"I'll be fine. But thanks for the offer."

"Then I guess this is good night."

"Call the office in the morning and let Brenda know what time you'll be arriving."

"Sure."

She started to roll up her window.

"Are you going to tell me how you know Ashford and Simpson, or are you going to leave me in suspense?"

Her smile took on a mischievous glint.

"Suspense is a good thing. Keeps the

adrenaline going," she teased. "I'm sure there are tons of secrets you have."

His gaze zeroed in on her face. "Maybe I'll share them with you one day."

Her stomach took a wild leap when the sudden depth of his tone reached down inside of her again. She swallowed.

"Good night."

"Good night, Dee."

She pulled off. Quick. Not sure what would have happened if she'd stayed a second longer. But what reality didn't provide, her imagination substituted as she thought of Garrett Lawrence and all the possibilities the entire drive home and through the night.

CHAPTER 10

"It's not cool what you're doing, man," Jason warned as he maneuvered the Ford Explorer that they used to transport equipment through the midday traffic. "Even thinking about getting involved with a client is bad business. If it got out, we could blow the grant. And need I remind you that we desperately need new equipment — equipment that we're planning to purchase with that money?"

Garrett glared at him from the corner of his eyes. He knew Jason was right, but he didn't care. Thoughts of Dione seemed to follow his every waking hour. Maybe they did have some philosophical differences, but it didn't stop him from liking her. He wanted to know her better. But Jason was right, it wasn't worth the risk. Besides she hadn't given him any reason to think she was interested. Hmm, maybe that was the turn on.

"Yeah, yeah," Garrett grumbled.

"At least wait until the project is over. If it's about anything it'll keep."

"Yeah, but what about those falling bricks?"

Jason tossed his head back and laughed. "Duck."

Dione was going over the text that she'd written, working and reworking the words, wanting to convey in sixty seconds a lifelong dream that she couldn't bear to have taken away.

Her intercom buzzed.

"Yes, Brenda."

"Mr. Lawrence and Mr. Burrell are here."

"I'll be right up."

She was seized with an attack of nerves and she knew it had nothing to do with being camera shy. She headed upstairs.

"Hello." She looked at Garrett as she stood in the doorway and a charge ricocheted between them. She averted her gaze in Jason's direction and stepped into the room. "Good to see you again."

"You, too. All ready for your television debut?"

"Pretty much. What's the plan?"

"I thought we'd get some shots of the office, and the day-care space," Garrett said, trying to stay focused on the job at hand and not Dione's legs that were beautifully displayed beneath a mint green wool skirt that barely met her knees. Even in her "all business" attire and with her hair pulled back into a tight knot at the nape of her neck, she set his imagination into overdrive. Then Jason's earlier warnings echoed in his head. *Duck.*

"Let's get started then," Dione said. "You can hang up your coats in the closet behind Brenda's desk."

Brenda got up and pushed open the wooden sliding door and pulled out two wire hangers, handing them to Garrett and Jason.

With that little chore aside they followed Dione downstairs.

"Is that all the equipment you have?" she asked realizing that all Jason carried was what looked to be no more than your basic camcorder with a directional microphone attached.

Jason chuckled. "Yep. But believe me, this little baby is powerful. Gives you the same quality as the big studio cameras without the hassle of size. It even has a built-in monitor so I can see exactly how the shot looks."

"Modern technology," she mumbled in

amazement, opening the door to the day-care room.

They were immediately greeted by a wall of noise from crying infants, to rambunctious toddlers who darted around the room in what looked like a game of tag.

"I'd love to get a shot of this. As is," Jason said. He balanced the handheld camera against his shoulder.

"Why don't you just walk into the room, Dione," Garrett instructed. "Look around as if you were giving a tour."

She heard that intense, focused note in his voice again.

She took a breath and stepped into the room, following Garrett's instructions. At first her heart was thumping so loudly she'd bet money they were picking up the beat on the microphone. Then she started getting into it, loosening up as she talked with Betsy who was bottle-feeding one of the babies.

The whole thing probably took about ten minutes and she was stunned to hear they'd probably only use about five seconds of footage.

"Why?" she asked a bit undone after what she thought was a stunning performance on her part.

Garrett smiled. "It has nothing to do with you," he assured. "We want to get a variety of shots. You'll be doing the v.o.'s — voice overs," he clarified when she frowned. "Then we'll come back to you at the end. Now let's get some shots of you in the main office, then your office and maybe something in one of the apartments."

She wasn't accustomed to people coming into her space and telling her what to do. And she was pretty sure she didn't like it. She cut Garrett a look, which he missed, while he talked to Jason about what he wanted.

She wanted to be annoyed at his "I'm in charge" attitude. She wanted to feel put upon and maybe a tiny part of her did. But actually she was intrigued by his in-control, challenging behavior. She could tell he was in his element. In the zone as the kids would say. Again she saw and felt his passion and for a moment they were on level ground.

What would only be a sixty-second public service announcement, had taken a full day to shoot and would take several days to edit. Just being a part of, and watching the process, was exciting, but Dione quickly understood the mammoth task of what putting together an hour-long tape and everything that went into getting it ready for viewing would take.

Dione was on pins and needles waiting for Garrett to call and say it was finished. She kept having this recurring vision that she was going to come across like the guy who does the Champion commercials. "When your bank says no, Champion says yes." Then he gives the worst smile as if it pained him to tell people he would give them money.

If she came across like that, she would simply die. That's all there was to it.

She tucked a stray strand of hair behind her ear then toyed with the gold hoop in her earlobe. She'd thought about Garrett a lot since she'd last seen him, the strange, almost sensual kind of closeness they'd developed as they worked together with him guiding and coaching her as she read her lines, turned toward the camera or moved around the building.

"Yes, just like that," he would encourage in a heavy whisper. "A little more to the left. Yeah. Let me see that smile. That's it." It was like an erotic, verbal game of foreplay.

A hot flash streaked through her. She shook her head, scattering the thoughts, but the feeling which had, against her will, burrowed beneath the surface, refused to go away.

Faintly she heard the front door buzzer

and the distinct rumble of a male voice —
one which had begun to haunt her.

The first thought that flashed through her
head was that the video was so bad, he
needed to tell her in person.

Her intercom buzzed.

"Yes, Brenda." *Did she sound as nervous
as she felt?*

"Mr. Lawrence is here to see you."

"Uh, you can send him down." Quickly
she looked around the small space, straightened her desk, smoothed her hair into place
and returned several files to the cabinet.
Returning to her seat, she adjusted her
jacket and turned her full attention to the
computer screen, and couldn't make out a
thing in front of her.

She felt him before she actually saw him,
before she heard the short, sharp knock on
her partially opened door. Still her body re-
acted with a start.

"Hell-o-o," he singsonged, sticking his
head through the door opening.

She looked up, appearing to be totally
unaware of his presence.

"Oh, hi. I didn't even hear you. Come in."
She put on her best smile, hoping it
wouldn't begin to fray around the edges
when he dropped his bad news. Her eyes
darted to the rectangular package in his

hand, then casually back up to him. "Have a seat." She extended her hand toward the paisley padded chair at the edge of the desk.

Although the furnishings had been purchased secondhand, Dione had no intention of them appearing to look that way. The old, scarred metal table she'd camouflaged with a large fabric-trimmed desk blotter, color-coordinated with her desktop accessories: pencil holder, Rolodex and appointment book, which she'd purchased at an African crafts shop, were all covered in mudcloth. Of course she couldn't afford original art, but she knew a good frame purchased cheaply could do miracles for a so-so picture.

Captured beneath glass, gleaming wood and silver were ordinary landscapes and portraits of unimportant people all enhanced by some added creativity.

She had great taste, Garrett thought really paying attention to the room for the first time, as he sat down and absorbed the aura of tranquility that the room and Dione's presence gave off.

"So what brings you all the way over here?" she asked, hoping she sounded casual. She folded her hands in front of her to keep them from shaking.

She's always in control, never a hair or a

movement out of place or wasted. How long had it taken to get that whole image down to a science?

"Actually, I thought I'd bring this by in person." He put the package down on the desk.

To Dione it sounded like a nuclear explosion, and she felt the threads that were holding her smile in place begin to unravel. It sat there between them like a frog on a rock.

"Got a VCR? I'm anxious for you to see it."

"Really? Why?"

"You don't have to look at me like you think I stole the family inheritance," he deadpanned.

A burst of laughter released the tension that had held her captive from the moment she'd heard his voice from upstairs.

"Now that's more like it," he grinned. "I thought you were going to put me in front of the firing squad."

"Nothing quite that dramatic." She angled her head in the direction of the tape and wrinkled her nose. "Is that it?"

He flashed that dimple and his eyes crinkled when he smiled, she noticed.

"Is that why you're so tense?"

"I'm not tense."

"Hmm."

"I'm not," she insisted.

He held up his hand. "Hey, I believe you. And if you're even the slightest bit worried about the tape — well — you should be."

"What!" She popped up from her seat as if she had springs. Her heart was thudding. This was it. She'd made a complete fool of herself, on videotape no less. And there he sat smug as he wanted to be, enjoying her humiliation.

She covered her face with her hands then began to pace. "I knew I shouldn't have done it. I came out like that guy, what's-his-name from the Champion commercial." She spun toward him. "Didn't I? You might as well tell me."

When she stopped ranting long enough to focus on his face, she saw that he was grinning like a fool.

"What's so funny?"

"You. I thought a little payback was in order. You asked after dinner the other night what secrets would I have that you'd want to know."

She planted her hands on her hips, the challenging ninety degree stance kicking in. Then she gave him "the look."

"Okay, okay. What I was saying was that you should be concerned because after this gets out on the air, casting directors will be beating down your door."

Her eyes widened in confusion.

"You were great. You're a natural."

"Really?"

"Trust me. I have an entirely different approach when the talent is lousy. It's usually a phone call."

"You know you're an evil man, Garrett Lawrence. To the bone."

"I've been called worse. So — do you have a VCR?"

"There's one upstairs in the visitor's room."

He handed her the tape, then stood. "Well, take a look at it and give me a call. I know you'll be pleased."

"You aren't going to stay?"

"No. I have a ton of work to do."

"Oh." She was a bit let down but touched that he made the trip.

Was that disappointment he heard in her voice, or wishful thinking?

"But if you really want me to. I —"

"No. I understand. I probably won't get to this until later anyway. I'll just take it home and watch it tonight."

He nodded. "I better get rolling. Call if you have any questions or comments."

"I will."

He started toward the door, then stopped

and turned toward her. "We'll be here first thing Monday morning to start gathering footage for the documentary. We're going to try to get it done as quickly as possible. There are a bunch of questions that we'll need to ask and releases to be signed. We'll be doing some sit-down interviews with you and the staff and whatever girls have agreed to participate."

"Fine."

"See you Monday."

"Have a good weekend."

"You, too."

He walked out and Dione suddenly felt as if all the energy had gone with him. She looked down at the tape in her hand.

She'd watch it at home in the privacy of her bedroom. That way if he said what he did to spare her feelings, at least she'd be humiliated without an audience.

Garrett left after saying good-bye to Brenda. But he wanted to turn back around and ask Dione to spend the day with him tomorrow. That would be out of line, and he knew it. But, he didn't want to spend another empty weekend alone or with someone who made him wish he was alone.

He pushed open the door and stepped outside.

CHAPTER 11

Dione unlocked the door of her two-bedroom apartment. Each time she stepped across the threshold she felt truly blessed, remembering where she'd been and where she was now.

It wasn't luxury but it was aesthetically comfortable with a view of Prospect Park directly across the street, and if she went up on the roof of the three-story brownstone, there was a beautiful view of Manhattan.

She slipped out of her cashmere coat, her one extravagance, and hung it in the hall closet that she'd sprinkled with bits of cedar. She loved that smell.

Flipping on the hall light she crossed the short parquet floor and stepped down into the wide living room.

Every item she and Niyah, when she was old enough, had selected for the apartment had been done with care. She smiled, recalling the weeklong debate they'd had when it was finally time to replace her ten-year-old living room furniture. Niyah had insisted that black leather was the way to go and Dione tried to explain that it would absorb all the light in the airy apartment and they'd roast in the summer with the sun streaming in through the bay window.

Finally they agreed that Niyah could have a black leather chair for her bedroom, and Dione settled on a cool beige fabric with pencil thin streaks of brown and gold running through it.

She looked toward the mantel where a framed photo of Niyah's high school graduation graced the marble facade.

Pride filled her as it always did whenever thoughts of her daughter filtered through. Niyah was everything any parent could ever want. She was smart, pretty, had a strong sense of values and a genuine goodness about her that attracted people to her. She had her pick of boyfriends, but Niyah's focus had always been on school, getting her education as quickly as possible so that she could make her mark on the world.

"I want to be like you, Ma," she'd said as they lay cuddled together in Dione's queen-size bed, the night before Niyah left to go off to Howard University.

At once the words filled her with pride

and just as quickly made her heart race with anxiety. For her daughter, she wanted so much more for her than she'd ever had. She'd never wished for the struggle, the pain — even though Terri always insisted that what Dione had endured had shaped the woman she'd become.

Dione just wanted Niyah to reach her potential and blossom into her womanhood without the trials that had plagued her early years.

She knew that she'd sometimes overindulged Niyah, wanting to give her everything. Betsy had daily insisted, "You gonna spoil that poor baby rotten. She won't be good for nothin'." And in the next breath Betsy would be cooing, playing with and indulging Niyah's every whim. And Niyah had turned out to be an endearing child, an inquisitive adolescent and a giving young woman. Dione knew it was because Niyah understood that above all else, she was truly loved.

Sighing, she stroked the glass that covered her daughter's face, knowing that she couldn't bear to have Niyah believe anything otherwise.

Still clutching the package with the video-tape, Dione walked into her bedroom, kicked off her shoes and opened the padded envelope.

"Well, here goes nothing." She opened the smoked glass of the television cabinet and turned on the television, then the VCR and stuck in the tape.

Perching on the edge of her bed, she pointed the remote at the VCR and pressed play.

After several seconds, her voice, clear and strong could be heard over the scenes from Chances Are. She briefly spoke of the house's five-year history, and the goals of her program. "But without your help, the dreams of these young women and their children will never be a reality. Chances Are is about choice — making a choice for a better tomorrow. Choose to be a part of a better future."

The screen went blank, Dione released a breath and actually smiled. Pressing rewind she watched it again and again. It was good. Actually it was great. Just like Garrett said it was.

Excitement and relief flooded her, running through her veins like warm water. She wanted to call him and tell him how happy she was. She jumped up from the bed and fished through her purse, hoping that she had his business card. Even though it was after hours, he had left his pager number.

Two meticulous searches later, she conceded that she didn't have it. It was at work right on Brenda's Rolodex. She'd have to wait until Monday. It would have to be soon enough.

But she couldn't get over the momentary sensation of disappointment. And it was more than not being able to tell him how pleased she was. She actually wanted to hear his voice.

"Oh, well."

She popped the tape out and stuck it in the box, then back in the envelope and set it on top of the cabinet. She had to talk with somebody and the most likely candidate was Terri.

She dialed her number and crossed her toes hoping she was home.

Terri picked up on the third ring, sounding hurried.

"Hey, girl, what's up?" Terri greeted.

"What are you doing? You sound like you were running around the block."

"Actually, I was halfway down the stairs, heard the phone and couldn't decide which direction to go, then finally ran back upstairs to catch the phone in the bedroom."

Dione chuckled. "That's some story. But I didn't call to discuss your directional problems. I got the tape."

"And —"

"It's great! It's really good."

"You're not just saying that because you're the star, are you?"

"No! For real, it's good."

"So when can I see it?"

"Are we still on for tomorrow?"

"Of course. If I don't get my bike riding in once a week I'm a physical wreck. It's my only exercise."

She and Terri had met every Saturday for the past three years — except those times when Terri was out of town — to ride their bikes along Prospect Park's bike path. With their erratic schedules, it was impossible to join a gym. And when they'd hit the big 3-0, and gravity started working against them, the battle was on.

"Great. Come by here first. You can see the tape and we'll talk about it while we ride."

"Sounds good. I'll be there about nine."

"See you then."

No sooner than she'd hung up the phone, it rang in her hand.

"Hello?"

"Hi, Ma."

"Niyah! How are you baby?"

"Fine," she giggled. "I just wanted you to know that I'm definitely coming home for

Thanksgiving."

"You'd better be. Do you need me to send you money for your ticket?"

"Ma — I have a job remember?"

"I know, but that's for school expenses."

"I can handle it."

"Okay. How's everything going with your classes?"

"Okay. The poli-sci class is murder, but I'm dealing with it."

Dione smiled. To Niyah, murder meant a *B.* She'd always been an excellent student and had been able to get into college a year early as a result. "When's the last day of class?"

"Tuesday before Thanksgiving. I'll catch a train Tuesday afternoon."

"When you know what time, let me know and I'll meet you at Penn Station."

"I'm aiming for a one o'clock train, which should put me in New York about five."

"Wonderful. Can't wait to see you."

"It'll be good to be home. At least for a minute. You find a boyfriend yet?"

"Niyah," she admonished, feeling suddenly like the daughter instead of the mother. Niyah was always direct and to the point. Her honesty was often brutal.

"Well, did you? You need somebody, Ma. So you can get out and do something besides work."

"I get out."

"Oh, yeah," she challenged. "Where?"

"For your information, young lady, I just went out to dinner the other night."

"Get out! With who?"

"His name is Garrett Lawrence."

"Oooh, is he cute?"

"Niyah!"

"Well, is he?"

Dione rolled her eyes. "Yes. He's cute."

"That's a start. What does he do?"

"He produces videos."

"Get out!"

Dione laughed.

"When will I get to meet him?"

"It's not that kind of relationship, Niyah."

"Don't tell me, *it's just business.*"

"All right, I won't tell you."

"Ma, you're impossible. Do you at least like him?"

"I haven't given it much thought."

Niyah blew out an exasperated breath. "So what kind of business do you have with a producer?"

Dione explained about the PSA and the documentary.

"Get out! *You* on television. I can't believe it. You're so low-key. Were you scared?"

"Terrified."

Niyah laughed. "Well, I've definitely got to meet him now."

"And why is that?"

"Because any man who could get you in front of a camera and out of your shell, must be something."

She hadn't dated much during Niyah's growing up years. She didn't have time. When Niyah was younger, Dione was busy trying to finish school, hold down a job and give Niyah whatever free time was left. As her daughter grew older, and more independent, Dione focused her attention on working harder to save money for Niyah's education, and her dream for Chances Are began to grow.

The few men who'd managed to get beyond the barriers she'd erected didn't last long when they saw the competition: her fierce love for her daughter, her undaunting determination to succeed and her devotion to Chances.

Dione couldn't say she'd been lonely over the years. For the most part, she didn't think about it except when Betsy or Niyah reminded her about her lack of a love life.

But Dione always insisted that her life was full. She was complete. She had friends, her daughter, Betsy and Chances. She didn't need anything else.

She blew out a breath as she undressed for bed. She thought about Niyah coming home for the Thanksgiving holiday and her last comment as she lay curled in her bed. Yes, Garrett "Gary" Lawrence was something. What that something was remained to be seen, she mused, finally dozing off, the vague images of her first Thanksgiving with Niyah materializing through the mists of her dreams. . . .

Her public assistance check wasn't due for another week and all she had in her pocket was ten dollars. The apartment was freezing. The temperature had dipped into the teens during the night after tornado-like rain. Ice hung along the frame of the rickety window, the whistling wind banging mercilessly, seeming to be begging to get in and creep beneath the three patched-up quilts that covered her and her baby.

Dione's stomach growled from hunger and she mentally pictured the near empty cabinets and the refrigerator that held only Niyah's bottles, a half dozen eggs, and the loaf of bread she'd stuck in there to keep it away from the mouse who'd staked out a claim in their little space.

The radiators rattled, futilely attempting to pump some heat into the building. Aromas of food being cooked throughout the building seeped through the cracks in the wall, and beneath the door that didn't quite fit into its frame.

Her stomach knotted, and a silent tear slid down her cheek as Niyah stirred beside her.

For the countless time she asked how could her parents have done this to her — put her and, at the time, her unborn baby out into the street without a backward glance?

Some days when she was off from her part-time job at the supermarket she would pack Niyah up and take the number seventeen bus then the number forty-six back to her old neighborhood and walk to the corner of the block where she used to live, and just stand there. Hoping for what, she wasn't sure. Maybe that her parents would walk outside and see her, realize how much they loved her and the mistake they'd made, and take her back. Love her again. And love Niyah.

But it never happened and she usually went back home feeling more lost and alone than before.

For seventeen years she'd lived in the big, rambling brownstone, with her own room, plenty of food and almost too much heat in the winter. She had a backyard to play in when she was little and a safe block to run up and down on when she grew older. She had friends just like her who lived the black middle-class life.

Humph. And then she thought she was in love and she'd given away the one thing she could never regain: her virginity.

He was a sweet talker, Michael Thomas. He was f-i-n-e as all the girls would say. He was the captain of the basketball team and every girl in Stuyvesant High School wanted to "get with" Michael. But he only had eyes for Dione.

And just that one time during a spring break had changed her whole life.

She never even told him she was pregnant. Michael had a basketball scholarship to North Carolina University, and she wouldn't jeopardize his chances.

So she wouldn't tell her parents who the father was. And her father tried to beat it and the growing baby out of her.

Well, Michael made it big at North Carolina. At least until his junior year. It was in all the newspapers and the television broadcasts that NBA hopeful Michael Thomas and two of his teammates were killed in a head-on collision. The driver had been drinking.

When she'd heard the news, she couldn't even cry. Niyah was nearly three years old at the time, and she'd long ago expended her tears. At least a part of what she would tell Niyah over the years was true. Her father *was* dead.

Restless, she turned on her side and the images shifted, changed shape.

Now, here she was on her first Thanksgiving away from home in a one-room apartment with a baby, no food and a high school diploma.

She heard a knock at her door and would have ignored it if Ms. Betsy's insistent voice hadn't pulled her out of the bed.

Gently she eased away from Niyah's warm little body and tiptoed across the cold plank-wood floor, every other strip creaked under her weight.

She cracked the door open and Betsy came bustling in, her arms laden with a huge aluminum foil-covered platter of food.

"Knew you and that child would be hungry," she said moving past Dione and into what served as a kitchen. "Come on girl, don't just stand there. Set the table and wake that baby up so y'all can eat."

Dione, still standing at the door, finally closed it and moved toward the circular table. A knot built in her throat so big, so tight she couldn't speak. Her eyes began to burn as she took out two forks and placed them on the table.

Betsy opened the cabinet above the sink, shooed away several roaches and took down two dishes, which she carefully rinsed then handed to Dione.

"Come on now, 'fore all this food gets cold."

Dione walked around the wall that separated the kitchen and eating space from the bedroom to get Niyah who was wide awake and playing with her fingers.

Dione scooped her up and held her tightly against her chest, finally letting the tears fall. "Somebody loves us Niyah. Somebody."

Dione's eyes fluttered open. Her heart was pounding. It took her several moments to orient herself to where she was.

She was in her apartment, not a rooming house. It was warm. There weren't odors seeping through the walls or howling winds knocking on the window.

There was food in her refrigerator and in the cabinets. She didn't have to squeeze onto crowded buses and trains. She had her own car. Her daughter wasn't playing with a doll made out of old socks that Betsy had darned together. She was at Howard University playing with a book about politics.

A shudder rippled through her. She curled into a protective ball. It could all dissolve.

Everything could be taken away. And she could be that frightened teenage girl again, with nothing holding her together but thin strands of hope.

She couldn't go back that way and she couldn't open herself to emotions that meeting Garrett had awakened. Feelings, love, giving of yourself took you off course. And her path was set.

Wasn't it?

CHAPTER 12

The television screen went black.

Terri let out a breath. "I think you missed your calling, girl. That was great. Mr. Lawrence did a fantastic job. I'd like to use him myself on some of my projects."

Dione turned off the television. "So you can use it?"

"Of course. I'm thinking of some angles as we speak. But — I think better when I'm in motion. Come on, let's ride."

"I have an idea," Terri said as they pedaled toward the park. "Let's really burn some calories and ride down to the Promenade. There's a great bike path and the day is perfect. Not too hot. Not too cold."

"Girl, are you crazy? You know how far that is?"

"Yeah, about a half hour. Same amount of time we'd spend riding around in circles at the park. We can take the train back if you're too old and tired to ride back," she challenged.

"Sounds like a dare to me," Dione said turning her head toward Terri and grinning.

"Last one there buys lunch." Terri zoomed off, her dreadlocks whipping in the wind behind her.

Dione was hot on her heels.

Just as Terri had said, the day was glorious. The sun was high and brilliant in the sky warming their faces, embracing their bodies. Up and down the tree-lined, residential streets and commercial blocks, there were people out enjoying the fall morning.

As her legs pumped the pedals and they darted around and between cars, Dione felt exhilarated, free and suddenly filled with that intangible feeling — that elusive emotion — hope.

But the rational side of her knew that what she was feeling only stemmed from something tangible. Something she could see and touch. The finished product. And she'd witnessed Terri's wizardry with marketing and promotions. She knew that Terri got results. That's what she was feeling — reality. Because hope was only something for children, and those who didn't know better.

She knew better.

■ ■ ■ ■

Before she realized it, they were riding along the path leading to the Promenade in what was called Brooklyn Heights.

The old-world apartment buildings, doormen-guarded hi-rise co-ops and exclusive boutiques were definitely out of her price range, but she couldn't help but admire the cozy environment and eclectic blend of nationalities who resided there.

They biked along the path past the benches on one side and the railing that separated them from the East River on the other. Beyond was the mighty Brooklyn Bridge on one side and the Manhattan Bridge on the other.

It was from the docks below that the yearly Fourth of July fireworks displays were held, the brilliant explosions visible for miles around.

They pedaled leisurely now, taking in the atmosphere, inhaling the scents of hot dogs, pretzels with melted cheese and gyros from the street vendors.

Dione wanted to close her eyes, just absorb it all, forget her troubles, commitments —

"Dione!"

Her bike wobbled when she heard her name called. She slowed and looked quickly behind her. She blinked.

There was Garrett jogging along the path.

She slowed to a stop. "Terri, hold on," she yelled to Terri who had pulled out ahead of her.

Dione planted her sneakered feet on the gray concrete, bracing the gleaming red racing bike between her thighs that suddenly throbbed from exertion. As Garrett drew closer she realized she must look a fright with her undone hair tucked beneath a baseball cap and sweat running down her face in a steady stream. She didn't think she smelled too appealing, either.

"Hey." He grinned, flashing that dimple, and slowing to a breathy stop. "What are you doing over here?"

"My 'always-reaching-for-greater-heights-friend' Terri suggested we ride over here." She angled her head in Terri's directions, who was pedaling toward them.

He ran the sleeve of his blue sweatshirt across his forehead. "You live around here?"

"No. I live near Prospect Park."

"Whoa. That's some ride."

"You're telling me," she groaned, her muscles beginning to protest. "What about you?"

"I'm about three blocks down. On Henry Street."

"Impressive."

"Trust me. If I had to move into this neighborhood now, it would be impossible. I was sharing an apartment with a friend about ten years ago. When they moved out I took over. Been there ever since."

A friend, she thought. Male or female?

Terri pulled up.

"Hi," she greeted, quickly looking from one to the other.

"Terri Powers, this is Garrett Lawrence."

Garrett wiped his sweaty palms on the legs of his sweatpants. He stuck out his hand. "Pleasure. I've read great things about you."

"They're all true." She laughed. "So you're the producer."

"That I am."

"I saw the video you did. Great stuff. I'd like to talk with you about some projects I'm working on. Maybe they'd be something you'd be interested in handling. My husband, Clint, purchased a cable franchise several years ago and we have yet to do anything with it."

Garrett's mind started racing with possibilities. Clinton Steele, CEO of Hightower Enterprises! "Sure. Dione has my number," he said as casually as he could. "Give me a call. Maybe we can get together and talk."

"I certainly will." She looked toward Dione. "Um, I'm really beat, Dee. I think I'll call it a day. I'm going to take the train back. But you can stay if you want."

"That would be great," Garrett jumped in, not giving Dione a chance to say no. "I mean if you want to. I could give you a tour of the neighborhood. Had lunch yet?"

"No, but —"

"There are some great little bistros around here." He turned to Terri. "You're welcome to come if you're not in a real hurry."

She smiled. "Maybe another time."

Dione had the distinct impression that she was being set up.

Terri stuck out her hand again. "Good meeting you. We'll talk soon. Dee, I'll talk with you during the week." She leaned across her bike and pecked Dione on the cheek, then sped off toward the Court Street train station.

"Well." He turned toward Dione. "You certainly travel with a celebrity crowd. I'm humbled to be in your presence." He gave her a mock bow that made her giggle.

"You may rise, peasant," she said tapping him lightly on his bowed head.

He rose, smiling, and even in sweats that had definitely seen better days, and a sweat-streaked face, he was a sight to behold.

Her heart knocked, asking to be let out, held and caressed. She took a deep breath and shut the door.

"Are you finished with your run?"

"I am now. You want to ride while I walk — or we can do the two-on-a-bike thing." His eyes picked up the rays of the sun and sparkled, she noticed, turning an inviting shade of warm brown.

"Why don't we both walk?"

She angled the bike, bringing her leg over its center. And Garrett had a sudden, erotic vision that shot straight to his groin and throbbed for a moment before he could will it away.

"Good idea," he mumbled.

They walked along the Promenade in an easy silence until they reached the exit.

"I'm over this way," he said, pointing to their right. "Do you come down this way much?"

"About once a year for the fireworks."

He chuckled. "Doesn't everyone? That's when I leave. Can't take the crowds."

"That's what makes it fun."

"So long as you're not trying to sleep through it."

"Sleep through it? That's a time for celebration. That's what holidays are for, people getting together."

He shook his head in denial. "Holidays are a big waste of time. Just another reason to spend money."

She frowned and looked at him out of the corner of her eye. "Don't you celebrate *any* holiday?"

"No."

"Why not?"

"No reason to. I'd rather work. Which is usually what I do anyway."

"What about your family?" she asked as gently as she could.

His chest started to feel tight. "Here's my block," he said ignoring her question and Dione knew the subject was closed. "Come on up. Get something cool to drink then we can grab something to eat if you want." He stopped in front of a redbrick building with floor-to-ceiling windows on each of the three floors.

"Okay." She pointed a warning finger at him. "As long as you promise not to shower and change clothes. If I have to go out in public all funky, I'm not doing it by myself."

Garrett broke out laughing. "Deal."

He took her bike and hoisted it over his shoulder, then trotted up the sandstone steps as easily as if he were only carrying a loaf of bread.

Dione followed in pleasant awe.

"I'm right on this floor," he said parking her bike beneath a huge mantel in the long hallway, passing a door in the hall, then walking its length to the imposing mahogany door at the end. He unlocked the door and stepped aside to let her pass.

"Welcome to the cave," he said in a sweeping motion.

"The cave?" She smiled.

"My hideaway. I can come here and hibernate. Come on in."

Dione stepped inside, directly into a huge eat-in kitchen with a rectangular butcher block table and four matching chairs that sat in the center of the room. All along the walls were gleaming wood cabinets, and little nooks. The stove was immaculately clean and she wondered if he used it, or if he ate out a lot. A microwave was tucked into a corner next to a washer/dryer unit. From the window she could see that he had a deck, the table and chairs covered with plastic. She wondered if he entertained much.

"The living room is this way." He led her through a door that opened to the front and she would have sworn she'd stepped into an electronics studio.

Lining the walls, high up on shelves, were two monitors, like the ones at his studio, a reel-to-reel and a very expensive-looking stereo system. Not to mention the flat, movie screen-like television built into the wall. He had a black leather sofa and matching loveseat. It made her smile and think of Niyah.

Since the living room was situated between the kitchen and the room beyond it, it had no direct sunlight, but he compensated for that by installing track lighting around the perimeter of the room and painting the walls a dove gray.

"Just a little interested in electronics, I see," Dione quipped.

"My one vice."

"This is really nice, Gary. What's back there?" She pointed to the closed door.

"My bedroom." He looked at her for a moment and she felt her face heat. He cleared his throat. "I have some Snapple Iced Tea, bottled water, soda and milk."

"Water is fine."

"Have a seat. I'll be right back."

Gingerly she sat down on the loveseat, concerned about her damp clothing on his furniture. She perched on the edge of the chair, totally self-conscious.

"Here ya go." He handed her a glass filled

with water and ice.

"Thanks." She took a long swallow.

Garrett plopped down on the couch opposite her and stretched out his legs. "Relax. You look like you're expecting the place to get raided and you're going to have to make a run for it."

She dipped her head. "I just feel so —"

"Grimy."

She looked at him and laughed. "Yes."

"That makes two of us. But thankfully a damp cloth cleans leather." He leaned back, rested his head against the cushion and closed his eyes. "Anything in particular you want to eat?"

"To tell you the truth, I can't go in to a restaurant like this. I should just go home."

He opened his eyes and sat up. "I could order something. Everyone around here delivers."

She rose and so did his gaze. "I really should go."

Garrett nodded and stood up. "How are you going home? I know you're not going to ride."

"Ugh." Her reality sunk in.

"I'll drive you."

"You really don't have to do that. I can call a cab, or take the train."

"I'm sure you could. But I'd *like* to take

you home." He lowered his head and looked at her from beneath his lashes. "Please."

She grinned at his attempt at charm. "Since you insist."

The ride to her apartment was short, too short. Yet, this was the very situation, that just days ago, she'd wanted to avoid — being this close to him in the confines of his car, any car.

But here she was and it wasn't bad. It wasn't scary. She was beginning to enjoy the closeness, the mellow music from the radio that wrapped around them. She even enjoyed Garrett's off-key humming to a Luther Vandross melody.

They talked intermittently about the neighborhoods they passed, the oncoming winter. She shared some anecdotes about the girls at the house and the infants who came just months ago and were now toddling around, the progress of many of them who had finally returned to school, those who had moved out after their one-year stay and had gone on to college or work.

He told her about his second passion — music and his wide-ranging tastes. They both agreed that underground rap was detrimental, that Billie Holiday was their favorite jazz singer, and that Diana Ross should have won an Oscar for her portrayal of Lady Day.

"Have any favorite movies?" he asked as he made the turn onto the circle of Prospect Park and then down Prospect Park West.

"Hmm. I liked *Face Off, Soul Food, Love Jones, The Fugitive, Titanic* and *Wuthering Heights.*" She turned to him and grinned.

"That's variety." He paused a minute. "Do you — go out a lot?"

Her heart thumped. "With work and all —"

"Yeah, I know what you mean."

"I'm just on the next block, between First and Second."

Any minute now he'd be pulling up in front of her door. She'd get out and that would be that. But he didn't want the day to end at her door. Away from their jobs, what they did, they were relaxed. They laughed and even enjoyed the same music.

"Third building from the corner," she said cutting into his thoughts.

He pulled up in front of a fire hydrant, the only available space on the entire block. He hopped out and opened her door, then untied her bike from the trunk of his car.

"I can handle it from here. Thanks." She balanced the bike, then focused on Garrett. "I really appreciate the lift."

He shoved his hands into the front panel of his sweatshirt. "No problem. I enjoyed it."

Her gaze faltered. "Well, I'd better get upstairs." She began to push the bike.

"Dee." She stopped. "I was just thinking — maybe if you weren't doing anything special — later, you'd like to see a movie."

She felt hot all over and her stomach was doing that swirling thing again. "Movie?"

"Yeah."

She sort of shrugged, looked down at the ground, up the block then back at him. Her heart was racing. "Have anything in mind?"

He almost shouted hallelujah. "You pick. And I'll pick the place for dinner."

"All right. What time?"

"Call me when you're ready. Maybe we could catch an early show."

"You'll have to give me your number. I have it at work."

"Sure." He went to the car and opened the glove compartment, fumbled around inside, pulled out a seen-better-days business card and scribbled his home number on it. For a moment she had a crazy thought and wondered if he always kept things around for a long time. Clothes . . . papers . . . people?

He grinned. "It's in pretty sorry shape,"

he said, handing her the card. "But the numbers are good. My home number is on the back."

"Thanks. So I'll see you later."

"Definitely." He headed for the car and jogged around to the driver's side then stopped before he opened the door and leaned across the hood.

"Dee."

She turned.

"*This* is a date." He got in the car before she had a chance to respond.

Chapter 13

Walking up the stairs to her second-floor apartment, she wasn't sure if the thudding she was hearing was her footsteps against the stairs or the pounding of her pulse in her ears.

A date.

With Garrett.

An excited smile tugged at her mouth as she fumbled to get her key in the lock. She wasn't sure why she agreed. But —

There really wasn't time to think about it — and she really didn't want to. That would just give her a chance to change her mind. Instead she focused on running a hot bath to ease the tightness in her muscles and figuring out what to wear.

Steam rose in waves like the sun bouncing off the hot pavement at the height of a summer afternoon. Dione eased into the water, inch by inch, her skin rebelling, her muscles echoing a joint *ahh.*

Scented peach bubbles sat atop the water like playful clouds, tickling her chin, dancing across her knees, between her thighs. She leaned back against the plastic neck cushion and closed her eyes, letting the warmth seep down into her bones.

This was really no big deal, she mused, this date thing with Garrett. They'd been out together before, they just didn't give what they were doing a name.

But now that they had, it took whatever was going on between them to another level. What did he really want? What was he looking for?

She sighed. It had always been so hard for her to express feelings, share herself with a man. All through her childhood, she'd struggled to earn her father's love, to have him look at her with warmth and adoration in his eyes.

Being at the top of her classes wasn't good enough — being pretty, athletic, having nice friends, excellent manners. Nothing was ever quite good enough to suit Richard Williams.

So she finally found what she was looking for in Michael's arms. The comfort, the embracing, the being told how wonderful she was. At least that's what all her studying in psychology told her. It's what the professors outlined in the textbooks.

Yet, even with all the knowledge, the understanding of her emotional gaps, it didn't make things easier. It didn't make it easier for her to love a man for the right reasons.

So she stayed away from commitment, of opening up, of giving. It was safer that way because every time she found herself drawing close to a man, she'd see her father's face, that leather strap slashing across her, her father's face contorted in rage, as he demanded to know "Who is it?" over and over. And she would feel so worthless and dirty.

Dione slowly opened her eyes. "One day I'll get over it," she whispered. "One day."

More than an hour later she sat on the side of her bed, staring at the phone. She held the battered card with Garrett's phone number, took a breath and punched in the numbers.

He answered before the phone rang twice.

"It's Dione. You said to call when I was ready."

"Then I take it you're ready and if you can hold on for about twenty minutes, I'll be there."

"Fine."

"See you in a few."

Slowly she hung up the phone and felt the excitement popping in her body like dozens of bottles of uncorked Dom Perignon.

Getting up she went to the bedroom mirror to check her hair and the barely there makeup. She brushed her hair until it fanned out around her shoulders and then she teased her layered front with her fingers.

She looked at her outfit and thought about changing it. Maybe the wool and crepe pantsuit was too conservative. She searched through her accessories' drawer and pulled out a printed, rayon scarf to drape across her shoulder.

She blew out a breath and pulled the scarf off, just as the phone rang. Her first thought was that it was Garrett changing his mind.

"Hey, girl."

"Terri, hi." She breathed in relief.

"So — tell, tell."

Dione grinned. "Tell what?"

"Don't get cute. You know what I mean. You and dark and lovely."

"Oh, him," she said trying to sound casual. "Well as we speak he's on his way to take me to a movie and dinner."

"Now that's more like it. This I assume is *not* a business dinner."

"He said it's a date."

"And you say —"

She paused. "It's a date."

"Well, just enjoy yourself. He seems nice, Dee, and we all know no one's perfect. So give the brother a chance."

"I will. I think."

"Don't think. That's always been your problem. You think and worry too much, usually about everyone else, unfortunately. Just go with it."

"Yes, Mother."

"Fine. Be sarcastic. Just have a good time. And do call me and give me the details, girl."

"I'm sure there won't be anything to tell."

"I hope not!" Terri laughed. "Talk to you later."

"Bye."

Dione smiled and shook her head, just as the doorbell rang. Her heart knocked hard against her chest, then went off on a mad gallop.

She dashed across the room and peered into the mirror, grabbed the discarded scarf and draped it back across her shoulder.

The bell rang again.

She took a breath, brushed the invisible wrinkles out of her jacket and went down to open the door.

■ ■ ■ ■

Garrett bounced from one foot to the other.
Waiting.

He was so nervous he felt as if he was ready to pledge his intentions to an unbending father for the hand of his daughter.

During the time he'd waited for her call, and then during the drive over, all he could think about was making a good impression, hoping that the evening went along without a hitch. He didn't want tonight to be a flash in the pan, a one night event. He wanted it to be the start of something. And the reality scared him.

He'd never wanted to be with a woman in the hope of wanting to give of himself. When he married Gayle, he married because he was needy. He was young, struggling and carrying around the heavy load of his youth.

Gayle Stanley was cute, not too smart but she seemed to genuinely care about him. And that's all he needed, even though there was only so much he could give in return.

Although his marriage was definitely not made in heaven, realizing that Gayle only married him because of what she thought he was destined to become was more hurtful than accepting that she'd never loved him at all.

But Dione — her compassion and passion for everyone who came under her care — awakened all the emotions that had been dormant. He wanted to take the chance that maybe, just maybe, Dione would take him under her care and care about him, too.

The door was pulled open and his hopes escalated.

They drove to the Lincoln Center area in Manhattan. The upper-crust neighborhood was braced by hi-rise, high-priced co-ops, the Lincoln Center for the Performing Arts, theaters and an array of dressed-up and dressed-down strollers.

The fountain at the center of Lincoln Square sprouted rivulets of water that resembled a moving rainbow as the water reflected the twinkling lights and colors of the city.

After parking Garrett's car in the Lincoln Center garage, they had dinner at an intimate Italian restaurant on Sixty-Seventh Street.

Garrett was every bit the gentleman, and Dione felt like a Nubian queen from his attentiveness to her every need.

So this is what I've been missing, she thought as Garrett held her chair and helped her on with her coat.

They walked several blocks to the theater, jostled periodically by rushing theater and dinner goers who didn't give a second thought to cutting right between them as they walked.

"We can put a stop to this," Garrett announced, after being separated from Dione once again. He took her hand and tucked it into the curve of his arm. "Now," he grinned, "let's see if they can get through this."

Dione looked across and up at him, his eyes dark and serious even though his tone was light. A rush flowed through her, warming her, even as the chilly evening air moved around them trying to find a dark haven beneath their coats.

He smiled softly. "This okay with you?" He looked toward their joined bodies.

"Umm-hmm," she mumbled not daring to trust the strength of her voice.

Garrett pulled her just a bit closer.

Sitting in the darkened theater, their knees touching and fingers brushing as they dipped into the box of extra-buttered popcorn, was an exercise in subtle seduction.

Every touch, breath, movement was an aphrodisiac. Garrett felt as if his veins had become live wires, charged by Dione.

She struggled to focus on the movie. But she knew if there was a pop quiz afterward, she'd fail miserably, especially when the heat from Garrett's nearness, the intoxicating scent of his cologne scrambled her thoughts. She hoped he didn't want to discuss the movie.

"Are you in a hurry to get back home?" Garrett asked when they'd emerged from the darkness of the theater.

"Not really. Why?"

"I thought we could go for a drive before I took you home."

She thought about it for a moment . . . she should go home. "Okay."

"So, tell me something about yourself that's not in your bio," Garrett said as he got onto the entrance to the Brooklyn Bridge.

"It's not that interesting. I grew up in Brooklyn, went to New York University."

"NYU. Hmm. Big time."

She laughed. "Scholarship. One of my closest friends is Terri," she continued with a smile thinking of her tell-it-like-it-is friend. "I love jazz, lazy Sunday afternoons. I take my job very seriously and think I'm good at what I do. And last but not least, I have a beautiful, almost eighteen-year-old daughter attending Howard University."

A daughter. So she'd been married, too. *Wonder where he is, and what man in his right mind would leave her?* Chances are, it was her job, he thought, no pun intended.

"What's your daughter's name?"

"Niyah."

He smiled. "Pretty."

"What about you? Besides being an electronics freak. Any kids?"

"No. None. Got an ex-wife, though."

"Hmm." She stole a glance at him and saw that his features had hardened. A tight line was drawn between his eyes. This was another touchy topic, she noted, which was just as well. Family wasn't the easiest thing for her to talk about, either.

"How did you get involved with Chances Are?"

"Sounds like a question for the documentary," she said stalling.

"Maybe, but I'd like to understand for myself."

He made the turn onto the Brooklyn Queens Expressway.

They only have to know what you tell them, a voice whispered. "I did my social work thesis on teen pregnancy." That much was true. "As part of my paper I toured several of the shelters and 'homes' for teen mothers. For the most part, it was depressing. There were no programs or services in place to make life better for them. They were just places for them to stay until they were transferred someplace else, or taken in by a family member." She blew out a breath remembering those days. "I just felt if I could, I had to do something.

"As it happened one of my part-time jobs during college was working in a real estate office. I learned the business inside out, kept my eyes on the market. The building that became Chances Are was in foreclosure. I took it over after months of negotiations with the community boards and the block association. I had to convince them that the property values wouldn't be lost," she said, her voice laced with sarcasm. "Finally pulled it off. The rest — is what you see."

"Wow. That's some story." He glanced briefly at her and suddenly saw her in an entirely different light. "So your degree is in social work?"

"Yes. And adolescent psychology. I just received my certification two months ago in social work," she added. "Now I can go into private practice if I want. What about you?"

"Nothing quite as interesting as your alleged uninteresting story. Lived and went to school in Brooklyn. I spent about six years in Queens. That's where I met my ex-wife — Gayle. Got married when I turned twenty-one. I was a free man by twenty-two. Bounced around from job to job, like I told you at the studio, until I went into production."

"How did you get the studio?"

"Not quite as difficult as how you got yours. Saw an ad in the paper one day for a space to rent. Me and Jason had been doing a bunch of freelance stuff at the time, renting equipment and what not, so we pitched in, took a lease with the option to buy and the property became officially ours last year."

Dione smiled. "That's great."

"It's a struggle sometimes. I'm sure not as extreme as what you're up against, but we have to keep our client base full and revolving. Part of our income is from the yearly grants that we receive to do public service announcements. It helps to defer the costs when we work with not-for-profit organizations like yours. The rest comes from corporations and private clients."

"Diversification of income is so important," she said.

"Definitely. But, if you're a private agency and not funded by the city, how do the girls come to you? How do they know?"

She smiled. "Several ways, actually. Although we're not a part of the city-funded network of shelters, we do work closely with social service agencies, high school guidance counselors and group homes. They make referrals to us. However, because we're not mandated to take whoever is sent to us because we *are* privately funded, we can set our own criteria for admission and the rules under which they can stay."

Slowly he nodded, taking in the information as he pulled the car to a stop.

Dione looked out of the window and the twinkling lights of the Verrazano Bridge, that separated New York from Staten Island, spanned majestically across the rippling water. In the distance, like silhouettes, the towering buildings of the New York City skyline were projected against the near cloudless night sky. Stars dotted the heavens and the moon hung at a precarious angle like an old drunk man trying to keep his balance.

It was beautiful to behold, and she wondered when if ever she'd seen such an exquisite view.

"How did you find this perfect spot?" She turned toward him.

"It found me. While I was driving, listening to you, I saw it in the distance. Always the cameraman." He chuckled. "My eyes never stop looking for beautiful things to capture." He looked at her. "And since we seem to be sharing some of ourselves, I wanted to share this with you."

She didn't know what to say, and the look in his eyes, the searching, questioning look only heightened the flutter that was out of control in her stomach.

He reached out, slowly. His hand, warm and surprisingly soft, touched her cheek. His gaze followed, connecting with hers, holding her perfectly still. "I want to kiss you, Dee."

What do you say when a man tells you that?

She didn't have to respond. Garrett took the decision out of her hands.

By degrees he leaned closer, unbuckling his seat belt, then hers. His eyes skipped like a stone on water across her face, his fingers threading through her hair, gently pulling her closer.

"If you say no, I'll stop," he uttered, a breath away from touching her mouth, so close that she could feel the tingle on her lips. "No news is good news," he said deep in his throat.

His mouth touched down on hers, once, twice, testing, teasing like a bee flitting from one flower to the next.

And then he was all there, fused with her, gently coaxing her into accepting what he had to offer.

Tentatively the tips of their tongues met like two pinpoints of light shooting electric sparks through their veins.

Her sigh enticed him, encouraged him. He drew closer, delved deeper and she gave of herself in return.

Those few precious moments of awakening, discovering each other brought them to a place where they had both feared to go. The place where decisions about themselves and where they wanted what was happening between them to go.

Garrett eased back. Slowly withdrew.

"I could get used to that," he said, his voice thick.

Dione lowered her gaze and bit back a smile.

He brushed the pad of his thumb across her lips. "You okay?" he gently asked.

She nodded. "I'd better get home, though."

He looked at her, trying to gauge her emotions, but she seemed to have shut down like the final curtain of a stage play.

A wave of apprehension swept through him and stayed with him like an unwelcome guest through the entire drive back to her apartment, intermittently given a reprieve with stilted comments about the city's landmarks and the weather.

He pulled to a stop in front of her building and double-parked next to a black minivan. Immediately he turned to her, almost sure that she was ready to bolt.

"Dee, I really had a great time this evening."

"So did I."

She smiled and the tightness in his stomach began to ease.

"I'd like to see you again — on another date." He smiled, hopeful, his dimple deepening.

"Garrett — I really had a nice time, and — but I don't think we should take this any further. It would just complicate things."

He felt like a fool. "Hey, no problem. You're probably right — mixing business —" He stared straight ahead.

"Well, good night. And thanks again."

"Sure."

She unbuckled her belt and got out.

Garrett waited until he heard the door to her building open and close, then he pulled off.

Now he remembered why he didn't put

himself on the line. Dione Williams gave him a quick refresher course.

CHAPTER 14

"Garrett Lawrence called a few minutes ago," Brenda said as Dione walked into the office to hang up her coat.

She felt her heart begin to race. "Oh. What did he say?" She took a hanger from the closet.

"He said the film crew would be here tomorrow morning to start shooting the documentary."

The racing intensified. She hadn't spoken to him since that night nearly a week ago. She'd wanted to call, but better judgment had overruled her feelings. She could care about Gary, really care about him and she was afraid of what caring would do to her.

"Fine. I was wondering when they were going to get started. With Thanksgiving in three weeks I didn't want the filming to disrupt the plans for the house."

"Dee —"

"Hmm." She picked up the stack of mail

from the in-box.

"Are you all right? You haven't seemed yourself lately."

Dione forced a smile. "I'm fine. Nothing more than the usual."

"Hear anything from Terri about the PSA?"

"She's been working out a campaign. I hope to talk with her later today. I'm sure whatever she does will be fine."

Brenda looked at Dione's profile. Dione had yet to look her in the eye.

"Is everything okay with Niyah?"

"Yes. Fine. She'll be home for Thanksgiving." She sifted through the mail that she needed to review. "I'll be downstairs." She turned and left without another word.

"Something's up," Brenda mumbled to herself and she had a strong feeling it had to do with Garrett Lawrence and her feelings were rarely off.

Tomorrow. She sat down heavily in her chair, biting on the tip of her index finger. What would she say? How would he treat her now that she'd told him it was strictly business?

Had the kiss they shared haunted him as it had done to her? Every time she closed her eyes she could feel his warm mouth against hers. She'd memorized his scent, the rhythm of his stride, the low throb of his voice.

Since that night she'd battled with her emotions, trying to convince herself that what she was feeling was purely physical. No real depth. But then she'd remember the laughter and the flashes of their pasts that they shared. She'd see the dark emptiness of his eyes that longed to be filled.

But she couldn't allow herself to fall for a man who thought so little of the girls and the cause she loved. If he felt and believed that way about them, what would he think of her if he knew the truth — the whole story?

And how could she even think of being with a man, building a relationship if it couldn't be built on honesty and trust. She knew from dealing with people every day what it was like when they carried secrets. It was in the eyes. She'd seen it in Garrett's eyes. There was a dark side of his life that he couldn't share, that had jaded him, just as her past had impacted her.

She knew that was just part of what drew them together, but it was the other part, the spiraling emotions that she couldn't handle.

She covered her face with her hands, wishing that when she removed them, the confusion would be gone and all the answers would be standing right in front of her.

"Dione."

Dione snatched her hands away from her face and blinked to clear her vision. She tried to smile. "Hi, Betsy. What can I do for you?"

Betsy stepped in, closed the door and walked over to Dione's desk. She stared down into her face.

"What's wrong, Dione? You've been a ghost around here for days. And don't tell me it's nothing, and don't worry. I'm not one of them girls," she warned.

It's nothing was right there waiting to make its pat statement. But Dione knew not to even try it with Betsy.

Dione blew out a long breath. "I don't even know where to begin, Betsy."

"How 'bout starting with how you're feeling right now and work your way back."

She pulled out a chair, sat down and waited. Dione knew from the determined look in Betsy's eyes that she wasn't moving until she was satisfied.

"Miserable. Confused. Lonely. How's that for starters?" she said, her voice beginning to wobble.

"Caused by something or someone?"

"Both."

"Talking to you is still just like pulling

teeth — a painful process. Ain't changed none in years. Keep too much on you and to yourself, Dione. That's what friends and family are for, to share your load. You'll be surprised to find it won't be so heavy. It's that man, ain't it? Must be because I ain't never seen you this down over some bills or lack of money or food. Just made you more determined. So — it's that film fella?"

"Still sharp as an ice pick, Betsy."

"So, I'm right."

Dione nodded.

"I'm gonna say these one or two things, then I'm gonna leave it alone. You got to give yourself a chance, Dione. I know all the weight and the guilt you carry around. You try to make it right every time you open these doors to a new girl.

"But you can't make it up. What is — just is. You never gonna get your daddy's love the way you wanted it, no matter how many girls and babies you love. You gotta love you first, then all that other stuff won't matter.

"They hurt you. Made you think you wasn't worth caring about. But you are. Give yourself a chance to be cared about."

"I — want to," she choked, her throat closing up. "I want to try."

Betsy stood. "Then just do it, like you done everything else you've ever wanted to do." Betsy turned to leave. "Got to get back to those children. Brenda can't stay with them but a minute before she starts getting panicky." She chuckled. "You come talk to me if you want. You know I'm always there for you."

Dione pressed her lips together. "I know," she whispered as Betsy walked out. "Funny thing is, I've been doing for others for so long, I'm not sure I know how to just do for myself."

Garrett had been as short-tempered as a lit fuse about ready to blow. All the guys in the office steered clear of him, thinking just the sight of them would cause Garrett to go off on them for some infraction or the other.

He barely spoke, kept himself shut away in the edit room and even Marva thought twice about getting on his nerves.

He was miserable. He knew he was being a real jerk to his staff, but he couldn't help it and wasn't sure if he even cared. But more than being angry, he was hurt. And he shouldn't have been. It wasn't as if he'd been deep into the relationship only to find out that the other party wasn't interested.

But his feelings for Dione had escalated at a frightening rate like a storm that was brewing, gaining strength and what everyone thought would be simple thunder and lightning turned into a tornado. He couldn't explain it.

He adjusted the dials on the edit board and the picture on the monitor above spun in reverse until he got the tape where he wanted it.

A knock on the closed door received a grunt of acknowledgment. He didn't even turn around.

"Gary, man, we need to talk." Jason closed the door behind him.

"Yeah, about what?"

"About your problem. You got everybody around here changing their underwear every time you step into a room." Jason grabbed a stool and straddled it. "I'm waiting. You're gonna have to tell me something."

"Just leave it alone, Jas."

"Not when it begins to affect this business. This is my business, too. Remember?"

Garrett shut his eyes for a moment and let the air rush from his lungs. "It's — man," he sputtered.

"Dione Williams," Jason said.

"Yeah."

Jason was quiet for a moment trying to find the right words. "Things didn't work out I take it."

"You take it right. Thing is, I'm not sure

why. I thought we were moving in the same direction."

"Maybe she's running scared, G."

"Dione?" He shook his head in denial. "Can't see anything rattling her. She's solid as a rock."

"That's what you see."

Garrett angled his head, looking at Jason from the corner of his eyes. "What's that supposed to mean?"

"Some things aren't obvious, G. People put on all kinds of fronts to protect themselves. You don't know what she's had to deal with."

"Yeah, well, I can't be responsible for all the brothers who came before me, either."

Jason slowly stood. "But that's what more than half the women you've run through have said about you." He pushed the stool back under the table. "Whatever you do, get a lock on your feelings. We still have a job to do and you two are going to have to work together for the next two months. Later."

Garrett watched him walk out. He should have just left well enough alone and never tried to take it beyond what it was. Just business.

"They're here," Brenda announced into Dione's intercom.

Dione felt hot all over and those crazy butterflies were going berserk in her stomach. How was she going to deal with this? The last time she saw him, they'd shared a heart-stopping kiss and opened doors that she'd quickly shut.

She stood, straightened her pearl gray Donna Karan suit and went upstairs. What they were about to get involved in was important. It went beyond her and Garrett's personal feelings. And she couldn't let her own wants overshadow that.

When she came up to the first floor, Garrett was coming through the front door, loaded down with equipment, followed by Jason and Najashi.

Their gazes connected and both of them seemed to become captured in frozen relief. Garrett was the first to look away.

"As soon as we get this equipment set up, we can get started."

His tone and expression were as distant as a foreign country. Dione's insides constricted, as she forced a smile.

"Is there anything you need help with?"

"No. But if I do, I'll let Brenda know." He looked away and continued carrying the equipment into the room used for the residents' visitors.

So that's how it's going to be. She spun

away and headed upstairs to check on Gina.

The entire morning and into the afternoon was an exercise in extreme agony. Dione tried to stay out of Garrett's way, which was impossible because everywhere she went to try to dodge the sparks that kept flaring between them, there he was; shooting footage, asking questions.

He had a smile, a kind word for everyone — except her. He charmed the girls, wrapped Betsy around his finger and even had Brenda laughing and smiling.

Finally the day drew to a miraculous close. They stood at opposite ends of the visiting room.

"I think we have enough background footage to get started," Garrett said to her as he packed his equipment, refusing to look at her. "We'll take a look at it, see what's usable." He opened his briefcase, pulled out a stack of papers and handed them to her.

"These are some of the questions I'll be asking, information we'll need." His eyes rose to smack with hers. "Hope *that's* not a problem."

She swallowed and stuck out her chin. "I'll review it and let you know."

"We'll be back tomorrow to get started."

"You expect me to go through all of this

today?" She could feel her temper rise and burn her throat.

"That shouldn't be a problem for you," he said. "All work. No play." His mouth curved up on one side.

He shouldn't have said that. He knew it the instant the words were out of his mouth and he saw the momentary flash of hurt flicker across her face and tense her expression. But just for that moment he wanted her to feel as lousy as he did.

He hoisted the bag with the camera over his shoulder. "Good night."

Dione watched him walk out and fought back the sting in her eyes. Why should she care what he said, what he thought? There was nothing going on between them. So what if they'd shared some laughs, some experiences — a kiss, and had somehow, mysteriously seeped into each other's souls.

So what.

She turned away, went downstairs and for the first time in years she shut her office door.

The following days that turned into the weeks before Thanksgiving didn't get any better or any easier. Every time they were in the same room, the same air space, it seemed as if they caused the lights to flicker from the energy they gave off.

When he came near her, coaxed her into the right position in front of the camera, eased her through her lines or sat opposite her while he asked questions about the facility and its beginnings, it was all a sensual experimentation with foreplay. The simplest word took on new meanings. A look, a touch simmered then scorched.

By the end of the second week, Dione was one jumble of frayed nerves and Garrett felt as if he would spontaneously combust if she touched him one more time.

He was just finishing up a brief interview with Kisha, who was being dutifully monitored by Brenda, when he caught a glimpse of Dione walking by the open door of the visitors' room.

"Excuse me a minute, ladies." He shut the camera off. "Just relax for a second. I'll be right back." He hurried out into the corridor, but not too fast.

"Dione," he rasped in a voice two notches above a whisper.

She stopped and turned, working really hard to keep her expression expressionless.

"We need to talk. I'll be finished in about ten minutes."

"About what?"

"I think you know, Dione." His tone

softened. "I'd appreciate it if you could make some time."

"I'll be in my office."

He nodded and strode away.

By the time Garrett knocked on her partially opened office door, she was ready to jump out of the basement window. She had a pretty good idea of what he wanted to talk with her about. It had been on her mind to settle the rocky waters between them herself. He simply beat her to the punch.

"Come in," she said.

Garrett stepped into the room and it seemed as if all the air had been sucked out.

Her heart started thudding harder by the second, the closer he came.

"Mind if I sit down?"

"Please do. What's on your mind?"

"Us."

She swallowed. "I wasn't aware there was an us."

"That's the problem. To me it seemed that's the way it was going. Then all of a sudden you pull a three-sixty on me and I'd like to know why."

She shuffled some folders on her desk, trying to collect her thoughts. "I have my reasons."

"Then tell me what they are and I'll leave

you alone — if that's really what you want."

"I . . . I just think we need to keep things — professional."

"What if I don't feel the same way? What if I want to take a chance and see where things can go with us?"

"Garrett, I —"

"Tell me you don't have some feelings for me, Dee. Tell me that and I swear I'll walk out of here and we'll never have this conversation again." He waited a beat. "I don't think you can. You feel it, too. Every time we're in the same airspace something happens. Tell me it's not true."

"I — can't," she finally said and felt as if a tremendous weight had been lifted off her spirit. A slow smile eased across her mouth. "I can't." She floated free.

Languidly Garrett rose and came around the desk. Her gaze followed him until he stopped in front of her, took her hand and gently pulled her to her feet.

"I don't remember ever feeling this strongly about any woman this quickly," he confessed, his voice low and penetrating. His eyes flickered over her face, followed by the soft caress of his fingers across her cheek.

A shudder rippled through her and she involuntarily shut her eyes as he drew closer.

"I'm going to kiss you," he murmured. It wasn't a question.

And when his lips touched hers, softly at first then with all the pent-up emotion he'd kept inside, she knew she'd been a fool to deny herself this pleasure.

After what seemed like forever and not at all, he eased away and they clung to each other, both unwilling to totally sever the tenuous connection they'd made.

"I have to pack up," he said, his voice thick and a bit shaky. "Do you have plans for later on this evening?"

She shook her head, afraid to speak, not sure what her voice would sound like especially with her heart lodged in her throat.

"How 'bout if I pick you up at your house about eight. We could go for a drive, have some dinner. Talk."

"I'd like that."

He grinned, feeling better than he had in too many weeks. "I'll even let you drive."

Dione and Garrett began to spend all their free time together and even that wasn't enough.

Dione, by degrees, began to feel that maybe this ray of happiness that she shared with Garrett would last — wouldn't be taken away — that she wouldn't be hurt because she allowed herself to feel again. That for once, she could receive joy and not feel guilty.

Just maybe.

"My daughter will be coming home tomorrow for Thanksgiving," she said as they sat curled in each others arms on her couch, watching a cable rerun of *The Godfather.*

His insides knotted. *Holidays. Children.* Both were sore topics for him. "Hmm," was all he said, stroking her hair.

She angled her head and looked at him. "What is it?"

He blew out a breath. "I'm not a holiday person, Dee. I hope you don't expect me to be around."

"Not even if it's important to me?"

"I don't ask you to do things you don't believe in."

She sat up and moved slightly away. "Things like what?"

"Like waste yourself trying to rehabilitate a bunch of people who can't be changed."

"Waste myself! Is that what you *still* think? You've been there, seen what goes on. You've talked to the girls, asked them all kinds of questions and that's still what you think?"

"Yes. That's still what I think. I admire what you do, but —"

Her entire body heated as the anger mixed with disappointment blended together into a potent liquid that rushed out like a geyser. "I don't give a damn about your admiration." She stood. "I should have followed my instincts from the beginning. I — can't be with someone who thinks so little of what I do. That equates to thinking so little of me in my book."

"One thing doesn't have anything to do with the other."

"It has everything to do with it. This was a mistake. Let's not multiply it by taking it any further."

"What are you saying?"

"Read my lips. I'm saying I think you should leave before something gets said that can't be taken back."

"Dee —"

"Please go."

CHAPTER 15

Seeing her daughter after months of separation was just what she needed to lift her sagging spirits. She couldn't remember if she'd actually slept. It seemed as if she'd laid awake watching the shadows from the street play games of tag across her wall, until the light broke through the night sky and scared the shadows away.

Her body ached. Her eyes burned.

What made her think, even for a minute, that Garrett was the one who could make a difference in her life? She was a fool to think she had the power to change his warped way of thinking. Even though she prided herself on the success of many of the girls, there were those whom she couldn't save, couldn't change. Garrett Lawrence fell into that category.

The stop-and-go traffic into Manhattan did little to soothe her raw nerves. Everybody and their mother seemed to be on the road and all going to the same place.

After an hour-and-a-half trip that should have been forty-five minutes, she finally saw Pennsylvania Station looming ahead. The one miracle of the grueling trip was that there was a lot across the street that actually had space.

Pushing through the crowds, and around huge and awkward pieces of luggage, she finally plowed her way through to the arrival area.

Peering over heads and trying to keep her balance from being jostled, she spotted Niyah coming up the escalator, and the weariness that had possessed her like an evil spirit was exorcised.

Niyah's face lit up with excitement when she saw her mother waiting, then just as quickly the light dimmed.

Something was wrong.

Dione stretched out her arms and Niyah stepped in, absorbing the long overdue comfort of her mother's embrace, then pulled back and looked into her mother's eyes.

"What's wrong, Ma?"

"Nothing's wrong." She pushed a smile across her mouth, and took Niyah's hand as they began to walk toward the exit.

"Who knows you better than me? Nobody," she said, answering her own question. "And I know when something's wrong. You look unhappy."

"No, sweetheart, really. I'm just tired. This whole business with the documentary, worrying about the status of Chances Are, has been a bit much lately."

Niyah tugged her rolling cart with her suitcase over the slight bump of the escalator leading to the street. "You're sure?" She glanced sideways at her mother.

"Absolutely. And I want to put all of that on the back burner and focus all of my attention on my child." Dione squeezed Niyah's hand as they emerged from underground. "I'm parked in the lot across the street."

Niyah listened but wasn't totally convinced. Neither of them had ever been good at hiding their feelings from each other. For years, Niyah and her mother were closer than sisters. Now that she was an adult, she felt they were truly friends. And with that type of closeness comes a sixth sense, a vibe that could be read as easily as A, B, C.

The vibe was off. But Niyah felt confident that whatever was bothering her mother she would get it out of her in the days ahead.

As they drove through Manhattan en route

to Brooklyn, Niyah took in the sights, the rush of people, the unbelievable traffic, towering bridges and the unmistakable charge that was unique to New York.

She sat back and smiled. It felt good to be home as much as she enjoyed being on her own, proving to herself and to her mother that she could take care of herself. She knew all to well her mother's struggle in raising her alone, the sacrifices she made to ensure that she had a good life. She knew much more than her mother thought she did.

Now it was time to take some of the burden off her mother. She wanted Dione to finally have a life of her own, to find some happiness outside of her job, to receive just a little bit of what she gave.

The idea that her mother had possibly found someone to care about and who cared about her made her happy.

"So how are things going with you and that guy, Garrett? When will I get to meet him?"

"You'll probably see him at Chances Are. He's still filming and interviewing," she said, and Niyah realized she'd totally avoided the first part of her question.

"Things are going okay?" she pressed, glancing at Dione.

"Aren't you the inquisitive one."

"You're not answering me."

"There's nothing to tell. I told you that before."

She knew that hoping Niyah wouldn't touch on the subject of her and Garrett had been futile. They'd always maintained an open relationship and Dione had encouraged Niyah to be open and direct. It was times like this that she regretted it.

"Things didn't work out," she said quietly.

"Any reason?"

"Differences in philosophy. Big differences."

"Like what? Chances Are, I'm sure."

Dione snatched a glance at her daughter. "Why do you say it like that?"

"What other reason could there be? It's always come between you and anyone who tried to get close to you. And before Chances, it was school, and before that, me. It's always something, Ma."

"My work is important to me. You know that."

"I know. But — have you tried to talk with him, explain things to him?"

"I thought we were making some headway. He's there every day. He sees what's going on and it didn't matter in the long run. He still has the same off-centered feelings about teen mothers."

Niyah frowned. The few men who had made very brief pit stops in her mother's life, never came that close to her work, which, Niyah believed was part of the problem why they didn't understand or could accept what she did and why. They simply held on to their prejudiced ideas.

But she hadn't met anyone who'd ever come through those doors who wasn't changed. Something more than just society's views was the problem with Garrett Lawrence.

Niyah sighed. Maybe it was for the best, she concluded. She knew how important her mother's work was to her and anyone who came into her life had to understand that and accept it. But when she looked at her mother's sad, drawn expression, she didn't really think that whatever had happened between her mother and Garrett Lawrence was for the best. She'd just have to meet this guy and see for herself.

"Niyah!" Betsy squeezed her as tightly as she could, marveling at the beautiful young woman who had blossomed from the tiny baby she once bounced on her knees.

Betsy held Niyah at arm's length. "Just look at you," she beamed. Then she ruffled her cropped hair. "What did you do to that head full of hair, chile?"

Niyah patted down her Halle Berry hair-cut, and grinned. "This is the style, Ms. Betsy."

"Style!" Betsy clucked her tongue. "Young people," she mumbled.

"You have your hands full as usual," Niyah said, scanning the day-care room and the five children under her care. "I don't know how you manage. Why don't you get some help?"

Betsy waved away the question. "I can handle it. Besides, I know your mama can't afford to hire no more help. 'Cause if she could, she would have done it," she added, with a sharp nod of her head.

Niyah sighed. She'd told her mother on more than one occasion that she'd take a semester off from school and come home to help out. Of course her mother wouldn't hear of it. Somehow she managed between the full-time help of Brenda and Betsy and a social work intern who conducted a lot of the mandatory workshops and prepared the girls for permanent housing — one of the major goals of the facility.

But for the most part, her mother carried the load, and Niyah knew deep in her heart that Dione needed someone with whom she could share her burden.

"So what do you think about the filming?" Niyah asked, knowing that if anybody had the real story it was Ms. Betsy. She knew her mother inside out.

"Them girls gave your mama a hard time about it at first. But Brenda set them straight right quick." She chuckled. "I think it's a good thing for the house. If it works like they hope it'll take some pressure off your mother."

"Hmm. What about the guy, um, what's his name, Garrett something?"

"Chile —" Betsy cut her eyes at Niyah. "How many times did I have to spank your behind for trying to get slick with me?"

Niyah fought down a smile. Next to her mother, Betsy was the closest adult female in her life. She was family. The grandmother she'd never known. They had their own special relationship and shared secrets that even Dione knew nothing about.

"Ask me what it is you wanna know. And I'll tell you."

"Still can't pull anything over on you, Ms. Betsy." She pulled out a chair near one of the changing tables and sat down. "What's going on with my mother and Mr. Lawrence?"

"Haven't met him yet, huh? He should be pulling in soon." Betsy shook her head in annoyance. "Your mother is stubborn and too full of pride for one thing. And so is he." She wagged her finger. "I can tell these things, you know." She bent down to pick up Denise's son, who was tugging on the hem of her dress. He lay his head against her shoulder, sucking his thumb as she cradled him on her hip.

"Things seemed like they were working out. Haven't seen you mother that happy since you graduated high school a year early. But something happened and she's been miserable ever since."

"How do you feel about him?"

"He's one handsome devil." She grinned. "But there's a sadness there that he buries beneath his work, just like your mother does. Both of them seem to figure if they can make things right everywhere else it'll make up for whatever's missing inside. I think they'd be good for each other if they gave each other a chance."

"Hmm," Niyah mumbled absently. "I guess I need to meet this man and see for myself."

Betsy grinned. "I see the look in your eyes, young lady. Stay out of grown folks' business. Been telling you that from the time you could walk."

"But, Ms. Betsy," she said as she stood, "I

am one of the grown folks."

"Heaven help us," she muttered.

Niyah went back upstairs and was walking along the corridor to the main office just as Garrett's Ford Explorer pulled up in front of the building.

"When I make some money, that's what I'm getting," she said, folding her arms as she watched the vehicle ease into a parking space.

"Going to get what?" her mother asked from inside the office.

"A black Ford Explorer, like the one outside."

She stepped into the office and caught the momentary stutter in her mother's eyes.

Dione looked away and picked up the pile of correspondence left for her on Brenda's desk. "Oh, that's probably the video team," she said in an offhand manner.

"Great. I'll get to meet him — them." Niyah went to the front door just as Garrett and Jason were coming up the steps. She pulled open the door.

"Hi. I'm Niyah Williams." She smiled brightly.

"You've got to be Dione's daughter. You look just like her," Garrett replied, amazed at the striking resemblance. She was a younger version of Dione with short hair. This had to be the perfect picture of what Dione looked like at eighteen.

"That's what everybody says. Can I help with anything?"

"I think we can manage." He stepped into the corridor. "I'm Garrett Lawrence and this is my partner Jason Burrell."

"Nice to meet you both. My mom is in the office."

"Thanks."

Two full sentences hadn't passed between them since the fiasco at her apartment. He didn't know what to say to her, or how she was going to respond.

"Good morning, Dione." He walked into the office and put one of the cameras on top of the desk.

Dione glanced up from trying to look busy. She gave him a tight, windowless smile. "Morning. I hope you won't be too long today. We want to prepare for the holiday," she said with more emphasis than he thought was necessary.

"I should be out of here by noon."

"Good." She looked away, afraid that if she kept looking at him, kept talking, she'd tiptoe back over that line again and he'd already proven to her that wasn't someplace she wanted to be.

He snatched up the camera. "I'll let you know when we're done."

"Hmm." She didn't bother to look up.

Garrett strode out of the room, nearly knocking Niyah and Jason over.

"Slow down, partner. Where's the fire?"

"I'll be downstairs setting up."

Niyah watched him practically stomp down the stairs. Although she had been chatting with Jason and asking him all sorts of questions about the equipment, her ears were glued to the conversation between her mother and Garrett. If you wanted to call what transpired between them a conversation.

Her mother's clipped tone told her plenty. She was trying to keep her feelings in check. She'd always done that whenever what she was dealing with was overwhelming or painful. She'd told Niyah once, if she kept a lid on her brewing emotions she had a better chance of settling them within herself rather than risk overflowing and burning everyone in her path.

Obviously something was brewing.

"Mind if I follow you guys around?" she asked Jason.

"Sure, come on."

■ ■ ■ ■

Niyah kept an eagle eye on Garrett: how he talked with the girls, how he coaxed them into being open and relaxed, how he worked the equipment. But most of all, she watched the dynamics between him and her mother each time they had to interact.

Her mother was more reserved than she'd ever seen her while Garrett talked with her about the program and her goals. But it was when Dione knew Garrett wasn't watching that Niyah saw the truth.

The way her mother's expression softened, and her eyes picked up the light. Her mother really liked him, but she was doing a good job of hiding it.

"That's about it for today," Garrett said, shutting off the camera. "Thanks."

Dione got up from the couch in the visiting room, said her good-byes and walked out. Niyah watched Garrett's gaze follow Dione until she was out of sight.

"Is the temp here yet?" Dione asked Brenda when she'd returned to the office.

"Just got here. She's with Betsy doing rounds."

"Great."

It was always so difficult to get help during the holiday season to cover for staff who wanted to be with their families. With the house being a twenty-four hour operation, someone had to be on duty at all times. The agency they'd been using since opening had been wonderful in providing reliable help to fill the staffing gap. And even though Betsy lived on-site in her own apartment, she'd spent every holiday with Dione and Niyah for the past eighteen years.

Betsy and the temp appeared in the doorway.

"Here you are," Betsy said, breathing a bit hard. "This is Christine Long. She's going to work the holiday shift."

Dione extended her hand. "Dione Williams. Welcome and thanks. I'm sure Betsy filled you in on everything."

"Yes, she did," Christine said in a slight West Indian accent.

"Things are usually pretty quiet for Thanksgiving. The girls generally get together and cook one big meal, which they'll have downstairs. Any problems or questions, my number is in the Rolodex. I'll be by sometime on Thursday."

"I'm sure everything will be fine."

"Okay, folks. Have a great holiday. Betsy, I'm parked out front."

"Be out in a minute. Just have to get my bag."

"I'll help you, Ms. Betsy," Niyah offered and followed Betsy out.

"Bren." Dione walked around the desk and gave her a hug. "Have a good one, girl."

"You, too. I mean that. Just relax and enjoy yourself, Dee. You deserve it."

"I don't know about all that, but I'll try."

"All ready," Niyah announced from the doorway.

"Christine, remember, any problems, call," Dione reminded her.

"I will."

It was just like old times, in Dione's Hollywood kitchen, only better. They weren't all squeezed into a small, cramped space. They didn't have to battle bugs and the cold. And they were together, laughing, joking, cooking and making a mess.

This was family, Dione thought as she watched Niyah teasing Betsy while she patiently tried to show her daughter the proper way to knead dough for the pies.

There was joy on their faces, a genuine love. Betsy had been the grandmother Niyah never had the opportunity to have, and the mother Dione missed.

She should tell Niyah the truth about

what happened to her when her parents found out she was pregnant — how they wanted no part of her, or her child; how they never answered her letters, or her calls and had eventually changed their phone number.

Niyah believed that her grandparents had died before she was born and Ms. Betsy had taken them in. She'd tried to give Niyah everything in her power as if it would somehow make up for the voids in her life.

Looking at her now, she was happy with the results.

Thanksgiving morning her apartment was filled with the scents of baking turkey, collard greens boiling in the huge pot, baked macaroni oozing with three kinds of cheese and Betsy's favorite: apple pie.

"Smells like a real feast for a king," Betsy said as she ambled into the kitchen. "Plenty of queens. Too bad there's no king."

Dione cut her a look. "Why don't you say what's on your mind, Betsy."

"All I'm saying is it would be nice to have a man around to say the blessing today. I'd like to see you settled and happy, Dee. I see how you are around that Garrett fellow. Holidays are a time to put bad feelings aside."

"He doesn't celebrate holidays," she tossed out, not meeting Betsy's stare.

"Maybe he never had anyone to share them with, or had anyone who cared enough about him to make him a part of things. You just want to see what you want to see," she mused. "Somebody who doesn't see eye-to-eye with you about that place is dismissed."

"Betsy, please —"

"No. You listen. For all your degrees and training, it's so easy for you to help others, but you can't ever see clear enough to help yourself.

"You spent the past few years of your life dedicating it to those girls, before that it was Niyah. But someone I know in my heart could be special and important to you, you won't give the same energy. And you know why? I'll tell you why, because in the long run it just might make you happy. And you still don't think you deserve it, that you should steal some happiness for yourself. You can't make up for the past by reconstructing everyone else's life. You got to work on you first. I keep telling you that. I've seen how he is with those girls. He treats them decent and with respect, no matter what other feelings he may have. And I see how he looks at you when he thinks you're not paying attention. It's not the look of someone who doesn't have some feelings for you. He's a decent man, Dione. A good man at heart. I feel it in my bones just as sure as I can feel a storm coming. If you worked on him half as hard as you work on those girls, you just might discover you've found a gem."

She turned and walked away, leaving Dione to her thoughts.

Sitting in her bedroom, with the morning moving toward afternoon, Betsy's words echoed in her head. She'd been staring at the phone contemplating calling Garrett.

She knew Betsy was right, and Terri and Niyah. Every single word. Somewhere deep inside she didn't believe she deserved to be truly happy. That to be happy would be a slap in the face to the shame she was made to feel, that had become engraved in her, a part of who she was.

So she lived vicariously through the joy of others, the success of her daughter, of the girls who came under her care.

Holidays are a time to put bad feelings aside, the voice of Betsy whispered.

Garrett sat alone in his apartment, the televised football game watching him. Would it have really been so bad to spend

Thanksgiving with Dione and her daughter? He took a long swallow of beer.

True, holidays had always been a difficult time for him all his life. Whatever foster or group home he found himself in, he always felt as if he didn't belong.

Holidays were a time for family and he didn't have one. Never did. He had no clue about his roots, what magical genes went into making him who he was.

He was nobody.

He didn't want to go through the rest of his life feeling that way. But he'd been afraid of what opening himself up to feeling would cost him.

He took another swallow of beer. Maybe that's just the way things were.

When his phone rang, he started to ignore it. He was only on his first beer of the day and he had every intention of getting drunk.

But the phone kept ringing. Finally he snatched it up and couldn't have been more stunned.

"I hope I'm not disturbing you," Dione said, trying to slow down the racing of her pulse with deep, silent breaths.

He sat up from his slouched position. "No. Not at all. I was — just watching the football game."

"Oh."

Silence.

"So — how is your day going?" he asked needing to keep her on the line.

"Hectic. But we've just about finished with preparations. We were going to sit down to dinner in about an hour or so, and — I was hoping you'd reconsider and join us." There she'd said it. Put it out there. It was up to him now.

The static vibrations popped back and forth between them.

"I'd need some time to spruce myself up," he said. "You know how it is just hanging around the house. I could be there in about an hour."

"Then we'll wait until you get here."

Garrett had been in Dione's for a mere five minutes and there was no doubt that he was welcomed.

Niyah entertained them with hilarious stories about her professors at Howard and the array of scandal in Washington.

Betsy treated him like a long-lost son, waiting on him hand and foot and he was loving every minute of it.

And Dione, what could he say about her? She was as regal as a queen at court. A vision to watch and he could see that she was in her element surrounded by love. Her face glowed and her smiles to him, small touches and whispered words of conspiracy about Niyah and Betsy all made him feel that this was the best decision he'd made in a long time.

It took all he had to keep the tremor out of his voice when they all sat down at the table, joined hands and Dione asked him to say the blessing.

Dinner was something he'd only imagined, seen on television, believed that it could only be for someone else. And here he was. The atmosphere was filled with laughter, lip smacking and the sounds of silver hitting china.

This is what he'd been missing.

Niyah insisted on doing her one last good deed before she returned to school, so she cleaned the kitchen and packed away all the food, while Dione, Betsy and Garrett relaxed in the living room.

Before long Betsy claimed fatigue and disappeared into the bedroom she shared with Niyah.

"Can I get you anything?" Dione asked.

"Please. No. I'll explode." He looked at her and laughed. "Dinner was great." He paused a moment. "It was better than great. And I want to thank you for giving me a second chance."

Dione looked down at her folded hands. "Everyone deserves a second chance," she said softly.

He stretched his arm along the back of the couch and draped it around her, easing her close to his side.

She rested her head against his shoulder and shut her eyes, allowing herself to simply enjoy the moment, accept the sensation of joy.

Yes, everyone did deserve a second chance, she thought sinking deeper into the comfort of Garrett's embrace.

Even her.

All too soon the day was coming to an end and she'd promised Christine that she'd stop by. Besides she wanted to check on the girls.

"I'll take you," Garrett offered, when she told him what she needed to do. "And no, you don't have to drive your own car so that it will be easier. I'll bring you back, too."

She laughed and looked forward to spending some secluded time with him. "If you insist," she teased.

Niyah and Betsy walked them to the door.

"Hope you had a good time," Betsy said

with a wink.

"I certainly did." He kissed her cheek.

"Maybe you'll join us for Christmas," Niyah suggested.

Garrett looked at Dione. "We'll see. But thanks for the offer."

Niyah reached up and kissed his cheek. "You make her happy," she whispered in his ear before moving away.

Their gazes connected and she gave him a soft smile of encouragement.

"I should be back in about an hour," Dione said, slipping into her coat.

"We won't wait up," Betsy said with a yawn and turned away, heading back to the bedroom.

Dione smiled and shook her head, feeling as if she were being sent out on her first date.

By the time they arrived at Chances Are, everyone was pretty much settled down for the evening. She checked in with Christine who confirmed that everything was fine, and she'd be turning in soon herself.

"Is there anything you need?"

"No. Betsy showed me where everything is in her apartment. And I brought my own personal items."

"Great." She turned to Garrett. "I just want to say hello to everyone then I'll be ready to go."

"Take your time. I'll wait here."

He took the seat Christine had vacated while Dione made her routine pit stops.

Everyone wanted to tell her what a great job they did at preparing their special dish for Thanksgiving and before she realized it, she was surrounded by the girls and their children who all wanted to share their day with her.

Her heart filled as she listened, seeing the sparkle in their eyes, the excitement in their voices, while at the same time realizing that she had been a part of making it possible.

Finally, the group broke up and returned to their apartments and Dione went back downstairs.

"Ready?"

Garrett looked at her maybe understanding for the first time just how important this place and the young women who lived there were to her.

He'd overheard snatches of the conversation from the floor above. The sounds of laughter and happiness. Dione changed people's lives — just as she was changing his. Those girls adored her, looked up to here. Whatever they were when they arrived, they were better now because of her dream.

■ ■ ■ ■

"Have I told you how glad I am that you called?" Garrett asked as he drove them back to Dione's apartment.

"No. How glad are you?"

He smiled. "Words escape me."

"Have I told you how happy I am that you accepted?"

"No. How happy?"

He stopped for a red light. She leaned over, cupped his chin in her palm and drew him toward her. "This happy," she whispered, sealing her lips with his.

In that brief moment nothing else mattered, not their pasts, not their differences of opinion, not old hurts. The only thing that mattered was how they felt about each other. Feelings that they couldn't put a label on, or try to analyze if they were right.

A horn blared behind them and Dione pulled away, laughing.

"Aw, let them wait," Garrett complained. "I was just getting used to that again."

"Maybe we need a refresher course somewhere else." Her gaze connected with his. "Maybe not tonight, but sometime soon."

He pulled out into the intersection, making the turn onto the Prospect Park circle.

"I like the sound of that. And until *soon* comes, we can spend the time digging through the debris that keeps cropping up between us."

"*I* like the sound of that."

"And I say we start tomorrow. How about if I pick up you and Niyah and we go to Rockefeller Center, spend the day?"

"Sounds great. One problem though, Niyah's going back to school tomorrow."

"But classes don't start until Monday. Does she have to go back?"

"You know how teenagers are. She loves visiting home, but she's had a taste of freedom and wants to get back to it."

He laughed. "Well you spend the time with your daughter and you and I can get together on Saturday." He wanted to ask her about Niyah's father; how he fit into the picture, if at all. But he figured there was enough time for that.

He pulled to a stop in front of her building. The lights were out on her floor.

"Looks like they didn't wait up," he said.

"Actually I thought they would just so they could interrogate me."

"Your daughter said something to me just before we left."

"What?"

"She said I make you happy."

238

Heat rushed through her.

"Do I?"

She swallowed. "Yes," she whispered. "You do."

"So do you, Dee." He reached out and stroked her cheek. "It's kind of scary."

"Happiness, or the fact that it's me?"

"Both."

"It is for me, too."

He took her hand. "Let's work on not being afraid. One day at a time. I want to try. Really try, Dione."

"Let's."

"You're standing me up for a guy!" Terri sputtered into the phone, trying to sound indignant but really thrilled.

"Don't be funny."

"Who's being funny? I'm being stood up. But I hope this is a pattern." She laughed.

"We'll see."

"Girl, pleeze. I can hear it all in your voice. You're just as tickled as you can be. I'm glad things are working out."

"Yes," she admitted softly. "So am I." She hesitated a moment. "I really like him, Terri. I mean I know it hasn't been that long, but — I just can't explain it."

"You don't have to. I've been there remember? Just go for it. Let it take you where it will and enjoy the ride. It's long overdue. Just don't forget to stop off at your local pharmacy like you tell the girls."

Dione laughed. "Thank you, Mother. I'll keep that in mind."

The idea of making love with Garrett had been dancing through her thoughts since the night of their first kiss, and had intensified every time she saw him. She daydreamed, wondering what it would be like.

Her brief sexual encounters had been just that, brief and unfulfilling. She wanted this to be different when it did happen.

"Anyway, have a great time. Oh, I sent the tape off to a friend of mine, Lisa, who manages a database of national funders and foundations along with some background on Chances Are. I also sent it to six cable stations. It should start running in about a week."

"Really! Oh, Terri, I just hope it helps."

"It will. Don't even worry about it. I'll call you during the week with an update. In the meantime, my handsome hunk of a husband just stepped out of the shower, maybe I'll give him a reason to get back in — in about an hour or so."

"Girl. I'll talk to you later."

"Bye."

■ ■ ■ ■

Garrett and Dione spent the entire weekend together exploring the city they'd both grown up in, but seeing it through each other's eyes. They went in and out of boutiques, tried Indian food for the first time, picked up a Kenneth Cole bag for Niyah, a floor-length robe for Betsy and a leatherbound organizer for Brenda as Christmas gifts. Dione weighed Garrett down with three shopping bags full of stuffed animals for the children at Chances Are.

Her enthusiasm and genuine pleasure that she derived from getting that something special for everyone, rubbed off on Garrett. He actually broke down and bought gifts for everyone on his staff, he even got a silk scarf for Marva. They dropped all the gifts off at Dione's house, stuck them in her closet and made a late movie.

And before they realized it, Sunday had arrived and their idyll was drawing to a close.

They sat in his car parked out in front of her building.

"I've had a beautiful weekend, Dione."

She let out a long sigh. "So have I."

"I guess you need to get ready for tomorrow," he hedged, not ready for the evening to end.

Her stomach started to flutter. "It's still a little early." She swallowed. "You want to come up for a while?"

CHAPTER 16

Even though Dione knew her apartment as well as she knew herself, she felt as if she were walking into it and through it for the first time. Everything seemed new, seemed to vibrate with energy.

She knew what she was about to do, what they were about to do, would irrevocably change them. Change how they saw each other, thought of each other. And she wanted it. She wanted the change. She wanted Garrett.

"Would you like to listen to some music?" she asked as he helped her out of her coat.

"Sounds fine." He took her coat, hung it up, then his while she turned on the stereo and put on Regina Bell's "If I Could." He walked slowly up behind her and slid his arms around her waist.

"We've done everything under the sun this weekend," he breathed against the back of her neck. "Except dance." He turned her around in his arms. "Dance with me."

Her heart slammed against her chest then settled as she moved into his arms, resting her head against his shoulder — so easy, so perfect as if this was where she'd always belonged.

"I would wipe away the sadness in your eyes," Regina sang.

Garrett held her closer letting the words wash over him as he cradled Dione, memorizing her curves, the slenderness, the soft fullness.

They moved so easily together as if they'd always been one movable piece. He knew this was where he belonged.

She raised her head, looking up at him, her eyes seeming to sparkle in the dimly lit room. Suddenly she couldn't breathe when she saw the darkness in his eyes, the unspoken words that danced in their depths.

"I think *soon* has arrived," she said on a shaky breath.

The corner of his mouth curved an instant before it took hers.

All of the air rushed out of her lungs as he crushed her body against his, became one with his. His tongue played tag with hers, darting, dodging, teasing while his hands roamed her length, caressed her hips, stroked her waist.

And then she felt his warm fingers sneak under her sweater to trail along her back. She shivered as the tips of his fingers toyed with her spine, up and down in long, slow strokes, along her sides until they found the curve of her breasts, setting her on fire.

She moaned against his mouth and he pulled her tighter needing to cut off the space, the air between them. He couldn't get close enough. He wanted her under his skin, to seep into his soul.

Their breathing seemed to rise with the crescendo of the music matching it beat for beat until they breathed one breath.

Garrett eased up her sweater, inch by inch and the cool air that hit her bare skin quickly became heated by his touch.

"Gary," she whispered against his mouth. "Come inside."

Reluctantly he released her, and she took his hand, leading him into her bedroom.

Through the towering windows the moon lit the room with a soft white, near-perfect light, just enough to cast a soft silhouette around them.

She started with the top button of his shirt, opening it, surprising herself with the steadiness of her hands, which Garrett caressed as he watched his skin appear beneath her fingertips.

Pushing the shirt aside, she ran her hands across his chest, teased the tiny brown nipples until they peaked. She surprised herself with her boldness. She'd never been that way with a man before. But with Garrett she felt new, daring, needing to break free of her self-imposed restraints.

Halting her exploration of his body, he lifted the hem of her sweater and pulled it up and over her head.

His stomach shifted when he looked down at the lushness of her breasts, full to overflowing in the mint-green lace bra. Deftly he unhooked it and slipped the straps from her shoulders, freeing her.

"You're beautiful, Dione," he uttered as the pads of his thumbs grazed the tips of her breasts, hardening them.

Her eyes squeezed shut when his mouth covered her right breast, drawing in as much as he could, gently suckling, his tongue teasing. A tremor rippled through her in concert with the moan that escaped her lips. Her knees felt weak and she clung to him even as he guided her back toward her bed.

Item by item he meticulously removed her clothes, slowly like an artist creating a masterpiece until she was bare and beautiful before him.

She wanted to scream at him to hurry, to

stop the fire that scorched her insides and rushed to her brain. But he took his time removing his clothes and preparing for her, and then he stood above her, the light from the window outlining his form and she was instantly reminded of an ebony god captured in the moonlight.

But Garrett wasn't finished with his leisurely pursuit of her. For what seemed a tortuous eternity he roamed across her flesh with deft fingertips and luscious laves of his tongue setting tiny, little fires along her skin.

"Gary —" She arched her body against him, needing the contact, the feel of his bare skin against hers. She stroked him, running her hands along the column of his back, memorizing the landscape of his skin, the smooth and rough texture of it. The feeling of his muscles expanding and contracting beneath her caress — everything about him excited her, especially the hungry, deep-in-the throat words he uttered in her ears, against her neck, between the warmth of her breasts.

Beautiful. So sweet. Need you. Touch me. Yesss.

Yesss. In concert they met, joined and became one perfect symphony, conducting the rise and fall, the frenetic and languid tempo with their fingers and mouths, thrusting arching of hips.

Garrett felt himself being pulled away, free-falling, his body no longer under his control, but Dione's. She had captured him, and with each tightening of her thighs he sunk deeper under her spell.

But in his soul he believed she wouldn't let him fall.

Heaven, she thought, as wave after wave of unspeakable pleasure flowed through her body, fueled with a new energy, creating its own natural high. For the first time that she'd been with a man since Michael, so many years ago, she didn't feel dirty or ashamed of what she was doing with Garrett, of what she was allowing her body to feel.

Her father's harsh, hurtful words had so traumatized her about the low she'd sunk to, she'd never been able to open herself mentally or physically to simply enjoy the pleasure of making love. Buried deep in her soul was the feeling that it was sinful and ugly.

But with Garrett, she allowed herself to enjoy her body — enjoy being touched, whispered to. The sensations that ran rampant within her were not ones of fear but pure and simple bliss.

When he whispered how good she felt to

him, how good she made him feel, she didn't feel like the "sneaky little slut," but a beautiful, desirable woman who could give as well as receive pleasure.

He took his time with her, guiding her, coaxing her mind and body to new heights, almost as if he sensed her doubts about her femininity, her womanhood. And because of his gentle, but steady pulsing persuasion to relax and release, she finally felt herself floating free of the restraints that had bound her.

"Come with me," he urged in her ear.

"Take me there," she whispered in return.

And the word games they played took on a brand-new meaning. The simple command and response brought their bodies into perfect sync, drew them nearer, closer to their ultimate destination.

Dione took the trip with him wandering over the valleys and across waters that she had no fear of treading. She seemed to see him just above the crest of the hill, waiting for her, holding on, reaching for her.

She reached upward in one last burst and he took her up and across the divide where she joined him among the stars.

Garrett marveled at the wonder they'd experienced together. Lying with Dione cradled in his arms he began to feel that all those other times, with all those other women, was to have this piece of perfection to compare the prior emptiness with. He pulled her closer.

"It's — been a long time for me, Gary," she uttered in a breath.

He was silent a moment while he stroked her hair. "Why now?" He felt her ripple with barely controlled laughter.

"I've been thinking about it almost from the moment we met." She laughed softly.

"You're kidding." He angled his body to be able to look in her face, which was contorted with merriment.

"You! Ms. In Control, always cool." His smile was slow and intimate. "Well, Ms. Williams you have made me believe in the saying 'still waters run deep.' What other little secrets are running beneath those waters?"

"Mmm. I was just thinking — maybe I need some more practice — you know just to make sure I haven't forgotten anything."

"Oh, believe me, baby," he uttered moving over her yielding body. "You could teach me a thing or two, or three. But —" he kissed her softly "— just to make sure . . ."

Awakening the following morning to find herself curved in Garrett's arms filled her with a sense of total peace. She'd been like the lone woman in the desert who'd finally, after an exhaustive search, found the oasis.

She sighed, taking a mental inventory of her body from the toes to the top of her head. Everything tingled with life, sparked by energy, and every unused muscle ached.

She smiled. But they ached so good.

" 'Mornin'," he mumbled, and tickled her stomach.

She swatted his hand away, giggling. "Good morning."

He locked his arm around her waist. "You weren't planning on going anywhere were you?" He nuzzled her neck and a little forest fire erupted. His fingers strolled up her waist until they reached her breasts where he stopped to reacquaint himself with their fullness.

All during the previous night, he kept waking up just to make sure the wonderful feeling of being with Dione wasn't a dream.

It wasn't. They were here. Together. His heart settled.

"We can't stay here forever," she sighed, a shudder rippling through her as he added fuel to the fire.

"I don't . . . see why not." He took a nipple into his mouth, gently flicking it with his tongue until it peaked.

Her eyes squeezed shut, a moan escaping her lips as her body rose to meet his.

"I guess we can," she sighed.

In the final weeks before Christmas they fell into a comfortable routine that seemed as if this was what they'd always done. After work, Garrett would come by and Dione would fix dinner, or he'd surprise her with reservations at a restaurant or for a play.

Some evenings they spent at his apartment and Dione would leave from there in the morning to go to work.

Happiness from the inside out was a part of who she was becoming and Garrett, day by day, was looking forward to all the tomorrows. And Dione was daring to feel that, yes, it was all right to be cared about.

One long, lazy Sunday afternoon they spent watching old movies on the classic movie station on cable. They even saw one of the PSAs that Garrett had shot and Dione was so thrilled for him, just bursting with pride to even know him, she hugged and kissed him as if he'd just won the Oscar. Sharing her joy, seeing his vision through her eyes lent a new significance to what he did. And he realized for the first time, perhaps, that he could make a difference, too.

They listened to Dione's treasured Billie Holiday album and concluded that "God Bless the Child" was their absolute favorite song.

"It says so much," Dione said, as the song came to an end for the third time. "You have to have something to work with to be able to help yourself." She blew out a breath. "That's what I try to do for those girls every day."

"Seems like they appreciate it, Dee."

She looked at him, trying to see if he really meant it, or just felt it was the thing to say. But what surprised her in his expression was not the sincerity she found in his eyes, but the sadness.

She touched his cheek. "What is it?"

He turned slightly away. "There's a lot I've been coming to grips with, Dee. All my life, even more so since I've met you and began working on this project." He took a long breath. "I want to resent what you do, but more so *who* you do it for. And for a while I did. I was able to push my own feelings to the forefront and the realities of what I was seeing, hearing and experiencing to the back, telling myself it was all just a fluke, maybe a front for the camera. I know it's not true. I've probably always known. But I've been carrying this — this hurt and anger around so long I couldn't bend my arms to put them down."

He paused for a long time and Dione thought he wouldn't say more. But when he finally did, the pain he felt became hers.

"I don't know who my mother is, or my father." His voice caught. "All I do know is that she was a teen who left me in an alley to die."

Her stomach lurched.

Slowly and deliberately he told her about the countless group and foster homes he'd grown up in, some worse than others. His feelings of rootlessness and insecurity, how he blamed the circumstances of his life on the girl who bore him and grew to resent all the others like her.

"I wanted someone to care, just about me. I wanted to mean something to someone. So I married the first girl who showed the slightest bit of interest in me." He took a breath. "I wanted to blame Gayle for our breakup and for a long time, I did. It was easier. It was always easier to blame someone for my circumstances. But the reality was, I was just as much at fault as Gayle. She used me and I used her. She married me because she had grand ideas about who I would become — some big corporate tycoon who would provide her with this wonderful life. And I wasn't interested in giving anything of myself. I just wanted to be taken care of."

He chuckled lightly. "After we broke up, I just ran from woman to woman — searching. And then I met you, the first woman who truly touched me in a place I'd never been touched and you represented the very notion that I'd come to hate." He slowly shook his head. "I couldn't reconcile the two things. Separate them."

He looked at her for the first time since he began to talk, and saw the tears glimmering in her eyes, sliding down her cheeks.

"I — I'm so sorry, Gary. I know how hard — how difficult if must have been for you."

"I honestly believe you do. If anyone could possibly know it would be you." He tried to smile.

"How did you find out about your mother?"

"She apparently got real sick after she had me. She wound up in the hospital. They put it all together. When I was older and was put into counseling because of my acting out in school and not getting along at any of the placements, I took a peek at my file. It was all right there in black-and-white."

She stroked his close-cropped hair. "So you did get to counseling?"

He shrugged. "It was part of my regimen. I saw enough counselors to write a directory. I can't say they helped. I know they didn't. Not due to lack of skill, but lack of willingness on my part to let them help. I didn't *want* to feel better. I seemed like that's what was holding me together — my anger. If they 'helped' to take that away, I thought I'd just fall apart."

He leaned his head back against the cushion of the couch and closed his eyes, wanting to block out the memories.

"What about now? If you're letting go of your anger, your resentment, what will hold you together?" She knew she sounded like the social worker she'd been trained to be, not the concerned lover. But she didn't believe that's what he needed, not now. He'd reached a plateau in his life. Perhaps their relationship was the catalyst, the turning point for him and he was ready to move forward. But he needed to be clear about that and the reasons why.

"I won't lie to you, Dee. I'm still angry. But I have realized, it's not everyone's fault. After seeing the young women at the house, hearing some of their stories that they were willing to share, the hardships that many of them endured just to keep their children, it slowly got me to realize that my mother is not the norm, not the one to set the standard. I only wish that she'd had a place to go."

"It's because of situations like yours that I started Chances Are," she began thinking of her own catalyst, wondering how her life would be different had her parents not put her into the street. Would she have turned out the way she did? Would she have felt the need for a place like Chances? She didn't think so. "Because of Chances, young girls have a safe haven, and don't have to endure the desperation that your mother felt. It provides some semblance of a future for them and their children, allows them to believe that their life isn't over, it has simply taken another turn and they must be prepared for the journey."

"Maybe if you'd been around then, things would have been different. But then you'd be too old for me." He gave her a crooked grin.

She laughed lightly, then sobered. "What happened to you and to so many others like you is what I struggle against every day." She took a breath, collecting her thoughts. "Chances Are is a necessary evil. You may not agree with its existence, but you can't ignore the reasons why it does exist, why it's necessary."

"No," he said, his voice thick. "I can't."

She laid her head against his chest, closed her eyes, lulled by the steady beat of his heart. Garrett had taken a leap of faith. He'd trusted her enough to unveil a part of himself, of his life that had been difficult and painful — had colored his way of thinking. The weight of the knowledge settled heavily on her spirit.

She wanted to be just as honest. Just as open. But the words wouldn't come. She hadn't uttered them in eighteen years. The only one who had a glimmer of what she'd endured was Betsy. Even Terri only knew just so much.

It haunted her. It molded her. It kept her from being able to trust those who claimed to love and care about her. Desperately she wanted to.

The words rose to her throat. The images danced behind her closed lids.

She swallowed, and opened her eyes.

"The way things are going we should be finished by the end of the week," Garrett said as he and Jason packed up the equipment at the end of their day.

Jason took a quick look around to see who was in earshot. "Is your relationship with Dione going as well as the project?" He glanced at Garrett.

"Better." He blew out a breath and grinned. "She makes me happy, man. I just — I don't know how to explain it. She's everything I could ever want. She's fun, intelligent. She has compassion that's bottomless and she accepts me for who I am."

"Bricks, man. I told you to duck." Jason chuckled. "But on the real side, I'm glad you didn't take my piece of advice about leaving that alone. She seems good for you."

"She is."

Jason clapped him on the back. "Be happy, G."

"That I am, my brother."

"I'm gonna start hauling this stuff out to the van." He tucked the tripod under his arm and picked up the monitor.

"I'm right behind you. I'll bring out the cameras."

While Jason went out to the car, Garrett went to look for Dione.

"Hi, Brenda. We're finished for the day," Garrett said, sticking his head in the office.

"How'd it go?"

"Fine." Garrett came into the room. "Betsy took us to each of the apartments and we got some great comments from the girls and shots of them in their living environment, cooking, washing, taking care of their kids. We'll take the next few days to look over the footage, see what we have and if there's anything else we need. If not, then the next and final shoot will be the Christmas celebration."

Brenda grinned. "That will be wonderful. We have a major surprise for Dione. But I've been sworn to secrecy."

He flashed his best "trust me" smile. "You can tell me. In fact, you should tell me so that I'll be prepared for taping — angles — all that stuff."

Brenda folded her arms and pursed her lips. "You know you have to do better than that. And even if you did, I wouldn't tell you anyway."

"I'm crushed."

"You'll just have to be."

He braced his palms on her desk and leaned a bit closer. "You sure I can't persuade you to at least give me a hint?"

"If you don't get yourself out of here —" she shot out, trying to sound threatening but she couldn't keep the smile off her face, especially with him looking at her with those big eyes and dimpled smile.

"Fine." He straightened. "Women and secrets — can't have one without the other," he mumbled on his way out. "And they're so good at keeping them."

Dione had been struggling with her conscience for the past few days. What Garrett had revealed to her about his mother had really shaken her, but at the same time it had allowed her to fully understand why he harbored such ill feelings and resentment about teen mothers — because of what they represented in his life.

She knew that in order to build a relationship it needed to be built on trust and honesty. Two major elements she'd been unable to live up to.

Everyone, Garrett included, had this picture of her, this "do good" woman who had her life in order, who had focus and agenda. She'd lived with the same illusion for so long, at times she believed it herself. But if she was as honest with Garrett as he had been with her, she knew she'd have to tell Niyah the truth. She could risk, she was willing to risk losing Garrett because of her inability to be truthful. But she would not risk losing her daughter's love and respect as a result of a truth that was best left buried.

Knowing these things, she knew she couldn't pretend to be building a relationship with Garrett. A relationship built on dishonesty was doomed to failure.

Her heart seemed to constrict in her chest, the right and wrong of her logic waging a vicious war.

She loved him. Heaven knows she loved him. And it was good she'd never told him. Said the words out loud. It would be that much easier.

"Hey, beautiful," Garrett greeted, stepping into the room.

The tightness got a stronger grip and she nearly winced with the pain. She forced a smile.

"Hey, yourself. All done?"

"Just finished."

He came around to her side of the desk, bent his head and kissed her cheek. He'd wanted to kiss her lips, see if they tasted at all like the berry color she wore on them, but she'd turned just a second before his mouth met her flesh.

A flash of unease rode through him. He reined it in.

"Everything okay?"

"Yes." She turned her gaze away, afraid that he'd see the lie in her eyes. "Just a little tired."

"Hmm." He walked around behind her and massaged her neck. "Thought you might like to know that we're pretty close to finishing. The only thing to shoot is the Christmas party," he said, his voice dropping a note as his fingers masterfully eased the knots of tension from her neck. Heat began to flow through her, even as she tried to keep it at bay.

"So you won't be needing to come back until then?" she asked sounding a bit too businesslike for his tastes. He dipped his head to the side to try to see her profile, gauge what it was he was sensing.

"Probably not," he answered, pacing his words. "Unless I think we need some extra shots."

She looked at her computer screen and the latest proposal she'd been drafting for the past week. She began typing in some additional information in the Program Outline section.

"What do you want to do later?" he asked, not liking the vibes he was getting.

"I — really don't think I'm up to anything this evening. I want to try to finish this proposal, or at least most of it." She wouldn't look at him.

They'd spent every evening and weekend together since Thanksgiving, as if they were trying to make up for all the time and the years they'd lost in not knowing each other.

At least that's what he'd thought.

Maybe he was wearing out his welcome.

He stopped rubbing her neck.

She kept typing.

He stepped back. "So I guess I'll talk with you later."

She pressed her lips together in a thin smile. "Sure."

He inhaled deeply, slanted his eyes in her direction then walked out.

When she heard his footsteps on the stairs, she hung her head, releasing the shaking breath she'd held. Her throat tightened, and that sinking sensation rocked back and forth in her stomach.

Her daughter, or the man she was in love with? Take some happiness for herself, or take it away from the one she loved more than life itself?

There was no choice. There never had been.

Garrett jumped in the van and slammed the door so hard the windows rattled.

Jason snapped his head in Garrett's direction. "What's with you, man?"

Garrett slid down in his seat, pulled his baseball cap over his eyes. "Just drive," he growled.

■ ■ ■ ■

She knew she was doing the right thing, the wrong way. She knew it in the days that followed and she came up with one reason after the other why she couldn't see him, couldn't talk too long on the phone, didn't have time to meet him after work or listen to Billie on Sunday afternoon.

And it was eating her alive. But she needed his feelings for her to erode, dissolve, not be fueled by some vain hope that things could work out, "if they could just talk about it." The truth was if she saw him, looked into his eyes, let his fingers stroke her skin, heard his voice for a moment too long, *her* resolve would erode, dissolve until there was nothing left. And she would be back in his arms again, giving in to the love that had taken hold of her and wouldn't let go.

But she'd always seemed to make a sacrifice for love. For the better good. She endured her father's beating for the love of Michael. She'd lived on the street because she loved the baby growing inside of her. She created the illusion of a perfect world for the love of her daughter, and Chances Are for the love of so many young girls who could have been her over and again.

So, what would make this love any different? For every love she'd ever had, she'd had to give up something, or some part of herself in return.

Garrett stared at the reel to reel slowly spinning, pulsing out the sounds of Sarah Vaughan that he'd had specially made. He leaned his head back against the couch, his legs stretched out in front of him, and took a long swallow of Corona beer. He could almost laugh as he watched it turn. How much was it like his own life — just spinning? Going in circles.

He wanted to jump off the reel and move forward. He thought that's what was happening with him and Dione. And then bam, out of nowhere, she'd backed off.

He blew out a breath. For days he'd been trying to figure out what went wrong. At what moment things had changed between them.

No matter what he suggested they do together, just have dinner, watch a movie, listen to music, go for a drive; she didn't have time, or she was too tired, or she needed to work late.

It was none of the above.

And there was no way for him to find out if she wouldn't talk to him. Maybe that's what she wanted.

Humph. She'd played him like a flute. Got him to believe, to have a change of heart about teen pregnancy. She'd opened the doors to Chances and let him roam through and absorb what it was all about. She'd gotten him to open up, tell something about his life that he'd never shared with anyone. And she acted like it mattered, like she cared. Now that she'd gotten what she'd wanted, she didn't need him. Didn't want to be bothered anymore.

Just like all the others.

He threw the half-empty bottle of beer crashing against the tape. Beer ran down the wall, landing in a pool joining the broken glass on the floor.

CHAPTER 17

Dione's telephone rang. She turned off the water in the kitchen sink, quickly dried her hands on the soft peach hand towel that matched the decor and picked up the wall phone.

"Hello?"

"Hey, girl. It's Terri. Turn on your television. Quick. Channel eight."

"Hold on. Hold on." She dashed into the living room and aimed the remote at the television, turning to channel eight. And there she was, giving a tour of Chances Are, talking about the importance of facilities like hers and the need for funding to keep it going. Her heart raced with excitement and a hearty dose of pride. And in the next instant, a wave of sadness swept through her as an image of Garrett, his voice, his words of encouragement flowed through her. She couldn't have done it without him. The commercial came to an end. She returned to the phone.

"Hi. I saw it."

"You could sound a bit more enthusiastic. It was great!"

"Yes, it was. Thanks for getting it out there."

"Who you need to thank is that man of yours. He did a fabulous job. I definitely want to work with him, seeing the kind of quality he puts out."

Dione was silent.

"Now that I've gotten that out of the way, you want to tell me what's bugging you?"

"Nothing. Really."

"Please don't make me have to come over there, girl. I've had a long day. But you know I will sit right up in your face until you tell me what's wrong."

Her throat tightened. She tried to blink away the burn in her eyes. "It's nothing —"

"You know Clint is going to be real pissed off if I get out of this sexy negligee I have on, put on my sweats, jump in my car and come over there," she warned.

Dione took a breath. "It's Garrett."

"And?"

"Well . . . I . . . things didn't work out."

"You want to be more specific? What things and why?"

"He — a while ago he told me some

things, about his past, his childhood. He was totally honest and it explained so much about who he is and why he had such ambivalent feelings about the house and the girls."

"And that's a bad thing?" Terri asked, confused.

"No." Dione blew out a breath. "I just couldn't do the same thing."

"I see." But she didn't see. Not really. For as long as she'd known Dione, she realized there were issues that Dione never fully discussed. Yes, she knew Dione was a teen mother and had gone to live with Betsy when she was eighteen after her parents had put her out. She never talked about Niyah's father, or why she never told Niyah about her grandparents or what she had endured in those early years. But what Terri could not come to grips with was why Dione was so reluctant to share her story. If anything it was one of success, even if it didn't start off that way. Over the years she'd kept her vow of silence. She never uttered a word to anyone about Dione's early beginnings. Because that's what Dione wanted. Yet she felt that what she did for the girls would have that much more impact if they all understood that Dione was just like them at one point and had gotten beyond that.

Dione never wanted to hold herself up as some role model. That wasn't her style. But her own guilt, her inability to get beyond her past continued to mar her future. She was still that frightened teenager.

"Dee, I don't know what to tell you. I mean, you have to work it out yourself. But I think you're making a mistake."

"It wouldn't be the first one."

"So your plan is to what, multiply it?"

"I can't do it, Terri. It's just that simple, not at the risk of hurting Niyah. I won't do it."

"Fine. Subject closed."

"Thanks for getting the tape on the air. I appreciate it."

"It's what I do," she said blandly.

"Are you coming to Chances for the Christmas Eve party?" she asked, wanting to change the subject and soothe what she knew wore Terri's aggravated nerves.

"Sure. When is Niyah coming home?"

"She'll be here this weekend. Just three more days," she added forcing herself to cheer up. "I can't wait to see her. I know it's only been a few weeks since she was here, but it still seems like forever."

Terri smiled. "I have to remember to pick up her gift. I think she'll love it."

"What is it?"

"A portable CD player. I know she loves music as much as you do, and everybody and their mother has a Walkman."

Dione smiled. "That would be perfect for her."

"Dee, I just want to say one thing. You can't go through life continuing to protect Niyah from its realities. I know it's a 'mother thing,' but it's not fair to her."

Hadn't Betsy said almost the same thing to her about the girls? She knew they were both right. But . . .

"I've got to run. I'll talk with you soon, okay?"

"Sure."

"Think about what I said. Bye."

Dione listened for a moment to the dial tone humming in her ear before she hung up the phone.

She wanted to call Garrett, to tell him how stupid she was to let go of what they were building. She wanted to share her load with him, ease her burden. But at the risk of losing the love and respect of the one person in the world who loved her unconditionally — she couldn't.

She turned away from the phone and went back to washing dishes.

The days before Christmas were always an

enjoyable time, full of excitement, laughter and cheer. Dione would put her entire self into making the day as festive as possible, purchasing gifts for the children and something really special for each of the girls; organizing the decorating party who would hang garland, tinsel and wreaths from every available space in the house, making sure that everyone's refrigerator was stocked and that there was more than enough food for the huge meal that they all prepared and shared together. Each year they would all go in mass to select the perfect tree and Betsy would work with the toddlers to create ornaments to hang on its branches. And Dione took as much time and effort with her own home, wanting to make it special for Niyah and Betsy.

During the holiday season, Dione was one whirlwind of enthusiasm. And Niyah immediately noted the lack of it the instant she walked into her mother's un-Christmas-like apartment.

Her hazel eyes, looked quickly around as she dropped her bags on the floor. She couldn't believe what she wasn't seeing. Sure she'd come home two days early to surprise her mother and get in on all the fun of preparations, but she was certain that her early arrival had nothing to do with the state of her mother's house. Where was the smell of evergreen?

She hung her spare set of keys on the hook behind the door and walked slowly inside. Maybe her mother had all the decorations in a box somewhere waiting for her to come home from school so they could decorate together.

After a thorough search, she soon realized that wasn't the case.

Niyah plopped down on the couch. Coming home for Christmas was the equivalent of being a little girl again, when she would run home from school, rush through the apartment and see the tiny artificial tree gleaming in the middle of the makeshift living room. The one bright spot in the otherwise neat, but dreary apartment. And her heart would run a race to the tree and try to sneak a peek at the brightly colored packages that her mother had tucked beneath.

Someone had stolen Christmas.

"When are we going to start decorating around here?" Betsy complained when Dione came into the child-care room to check on the children.

"I was thinking of letting you and Brenda handle it. Maybe appoint one of the girls to be in charge." She bent down to pick up

Gina's little girl Brandy. She kissed her soft cheek and twisted a wayward braid around her finger.

Betsy looked at her out of the corner of her eye. "Brenda! Since when does Brenda take care of the festivities around here? And you know I ain't got the time with these babies down here."

Dione put Brandy back in the playpen. "I'm sure Brenda can handle it."

"Why aren't *you* handling it is the question?" She eyed her suspiciously.

"Maybe I'm finally doing what you suggested and letting them stand on their own two feet."

"If I thought that for a minute we wouldn't be standing here having this conversation."

"That's my decision, Betsy. I need to concentrate on other things right now."

"Like that man, Garrett?"

Dione turned away. "That's not something I want to discuss. I've got to go."

She walked out of the room, into her office and shut the door. Something she never did. No sooner than she'd sat down her phone rang. Only two people had her direct line. Niyah and Garrett.

She hesitated for a moment, then picked up.

"This is Dione Williams."

"Hi, Ma."

"Niyah! Hi, honey. Where are you?"

"At the apartment."

Dione frowned. "I thought you weren't coming until the weekend."

"I thought I'd come today and surprise you. But I was the one surprised. What's going on? I mean Christmas is less than a week away."

"What do you mean?" she asked, stalling for time. She'd been so absorbed in her own self-pity she'd totally forgotten how much Niyah looked forward to the sights and sounds of the holidays.

"What happened, or didn't happen to the apartment? Where's all the stuff? This isn't like you."

"Oh." She chuckled nervously. "I just thought I'd do something different and wait until you got home so we could do everything together."

Niyah listened to the words, but to her ears they didn't ring true. "Hmm."

"When did you get in?" she segued.

"About twenty minutes ago. Ma, is there something that you're not telling me? You sound funny."

"Just overworked as usual. But I'll be fine. Especially since you're home. I'll fix something special for dinner unless you want to

276

go out. We could do that," she rushed on.

"I think I'd rather stay in, if you don't mind."

"Of course not. Whatever you want is fine with me."

"So I guess I'll see you when you get home."

"About six."

"All right. See you then." Niyah disconnected the call and immediately dialed Chances Are. Brenda picked up on the second ring.

"Hi, honey. You're back or on your way in? Your mom is downstairs."

"I'm home. Decided to come home early. I just spoke to my mother. But I really want to speak to you."

"Sure, honey. What is it?"

"Is something wrong with my mother? And you know you can tell me."

Brenda hesitated for a moment, debating about what to say. "I'm not really sure," she admitted. "I can tell you this — she's not herself."

"Hmm. Is Chances just as barren as my house?" she asked, taking another depressed look around.

"The Christmas spirit has not arrived."

"Is Ms. Betsy available?"

"I'll buzz her. Hold on."

"Niyah. I know you're not calling me all the way from Washington," Betsy chastised as soon as she heard Niyah's voice.

"No, Ms. Betsy. I'm home. But I wanted to talk to you before my mother came in."

"Oh." Betsy peered over her shoulder, checking for any signs of Dione. "It's that man. I just know it is," she whispered as she rocked Denise's son on her hip.

Niyah frowned. "What happened?"

"I ain't sure, but knowing your mother she probably told him to take a hike and now she's sorry."

"Why would she do that?"

"Getting too close."

"Too close to what?"

"To her. To the truth of who she is."

"I don't understand —"

"Niyah, honey, I think it's about time that I told you a few things about your mother. I ain't never been one to run from the truth. Always believed you needed to stand up to it at all costs." She clucked her tongue. "But your mama always believed she was protecting you."

"Protecting me? From what?"

"From reality. The real world."

278

For a moment, Betsy debated about the right and wrong of what she was about to do. She'd been Dione's mother, father, protector and confidant for nearly eighteen years. She'd been there to hold Dione when she cried for her mother, fed her when she was hungry and took care of her and Niyah when they were sick — stuck an extra dollar or two in her pockets when she knew Dione was between checks. And that life, that special relationship she'd developed with Dione and then with Niyah, was sacred to her. But sometimes you had to break promises to the ones you loved, simply because you loved them.

She took a long breath, sat down and bounced Denise's son on her thigh. "Now I want you to listen and listen good. I swore to your mama years ago that I would never breathe a word of this to another soul. Especially to you. It's time I broke my promise." She blew out a breath. "Your grandparents, they ain't dead . . ."

Niyah listened, stunned, for more than a half hour to a story she'd only read about in newspapers or heard whispered among the girls at Chances. Never in her wildest dreams would she have believed that her mother had been through what she did and was still able to rise above it. What was most telling was that for all her sacrifices: financial, emotional, physical and personal, she'd done it all for her. To protect her from the fact that she'd never been wanted by her grandparents. Those same people who had given her mother life had tried to beat the life out of her, then tossed her in the street like an old pair of shoes. Protect her from feeling that she was less than worthy, because Dione was made to feel that way, and therefore any child she bore. She never wanted Niyah to, in any way, feel responsible for anything that happened to them over the years because of a single decision she'd made one spring night. And even to keep Niyah from knowing, she had been willing to jeopardize Chances Are and lose Garrett in the process.

Tears ran unchecked down Niyah's cheeks. How could anyone love another person that much? But she knew now that it was possible and she was the recipient of that unwavering love.

"She thought you'd never forgive her for lying to you all these years, from keeping things from you. You're the most important thing in your mother's life, Niyah."

"I know," she choked, sniffing back her tears. "And it's time she realized that I feel the same way about her."

CHAPTER 18

"I think we have all the footage we need for the piece," Jason said to Garrett as he turned off the monitor. He rolled his neck and rubbed his eyes, which were red and tired from hours of staring at the screen.

"Yeah, looks that way. I'll just be glad to get this project out of the way." Garrett snapped on the light.

"We still need to shoot the Christmas party. That will give it the final touch. Jerk a few tears from the viewers." He chuckled and stretched.

"You can probably handle it on your own," Garrett said, getting up from the stool. "Or take one of the guys with you."

Jason frowned. "You're not coming?"

"Naw. Got things to do."

"On Christmas Eve? You? You haven't celebrated a holiday for as long as I've known you. All you do is work. You and Dione planning a getaway?" he snickered.

"Is that all you ever think about?" he snapped, opening cassette boxes and putting the tapes inside.

"What's wrong with you? You been snappin' and snarlin' like a pit bull for days and quite frankly, it's getting tired."

"Then why don't I just get out of your way. I'll see you later." He snatched his jacket from the back of the hook on the door and stormed out, slamming the door behind him.

When he got outside he was met by a bone-chilling drizzle. And he realized he'd left his cap in the office. He started to turn around and go back, but then he was certain he'd run into Jason and then he'd have to apologize, or possibly continue what Jason began. He wanted to do neither.

Holding his head down, which didn't help, because the water just ran down his neck, he strode down the block toward his car, cursing under his breath. He felt as if he wanted to explode, to lash out and hit someone like when he'd been a kid and he'd been taunted or was feeling unusually lonely. Back then he could beat people up, get his frustrations out and the worst that would happen is that he'd be sent to his room, or to the principal, or to a counselor.

He couldn't pull that anymore. Now he'd get sent to jail.

So what he'd done over the years was pour his frustrations into blinding hours of work, work and more work, to the exclusion of everything else. Then he took up jogging and when work no longer eased the voids, he ran.

He felt like running now and to just keep going. Watching Dione, the house, the girls on the screen for hours had been his own undoing. He'd convinced himself over the past couple of weeks that it didn't matter, that *she* didn't matter.

It was a lie.

She did matter. More than he'd wanted her to, and he was paying for it. What bothered him more than anything, seeped down to his bones and chilled him like the falling icy rain, was that he didn't understand why. Why did he have to keep paying for wanting to be cared about? Especially now when he was finally learning to care in return?

He turned up the collar of his coat and started to run, slowly at first, then faster. He ran right past his car and kept going.

Garrett was soaked and exhausted by the time he reached home. Foolishly he'd run through the rain until he couldn't run anymore and finally had come back to his car.

He started stripping out of his clothes the instant he closed his door behind him. Grabbing a towel from the closet on his way to the bathroom, he rubbed it through his hair.

"What was I thinking about?" he grumbled, already feeling the aches from the cold rain settling in his muscles. He turned the shower on full blast and as hot as he could stand it. He stood under the steaming water for a good ten minutes before the chill finally left his body.

Stepping out he heard the faint ringing of the phone. Wrapping a towel around his waist, he stalked into his bedroom and snatched it up.

"Hello?"

"Mr. Lawrence?"

His brow crinkled. "Yes," he answered with hesitation. It was too late for creditors to be calling and besides the voice sounded a bit too young yet vaguely familiar.

"This is Niyah . . . Williams. Dione's daughter."

His stomach knotted. "Hi. How are you?"

"Fine. I'll get right to the point of my call. I know this may be out of line, but if I don't do it, I know my mother never will."

He rubbed his head with the towel and sat down on the end of the bed. "I'm listening."

"I don't know what happened between the two of you, and it's probably none of my business. But what is my business is my mother's happiness and right now she's not happy, and I know it has to do with you."

"Me?"

"Yes. My mother is a very proud woman, Mr. Lawrence. And that makes her stubborn. She spends so much time trying to do the right thing for everyone else she forgets about herself."

Garrett twisted his mouth as he listened, not really wanting to hear it, but trying to be polite. "Go on."

"I want to do something special for her."

"What's that got to do with me?"

"I'd like you to be there. I know you're planning on shooting the Christmas Eve party —"

"I wasn't planning on coming. Jason is going to shoot the final footage."

"I know I'm in no position to ask favors of you, Mr. Lawrence. But please be there. If you ever cared about my mother, please just come. It's important."

"I can't make any promises, Niyah. Your

mother, we — let's just say I can't make any promises."

She blew out a breath in frustration. "At least think about it."

"Yeah. I'll think about it."

"Thanks. Good night."

"Good night."

Slowly Garrett hung up the phone. Why would he want to do anything special for Dione after the way she'd simply dismissed him from her life? Bet her daughter didn't know about that.

He stretched out on the bed and stared up at the ceiling. *If you ever cared about my mother, please come,* Niyah's voice echoed.

"I still do," he uttered in answer. "But I won't put myself through that again. Not even for Dione."

By the time Dione arrived at her house, the rain had turned to a driving, icy sleet. Just the short walk from the car to the house had chilled her to her soul. When she walked into the warmth of her apartment that welcomed and wrapped around her like a down comforter, and to the smell of chicken baking in the oven, her entire body gave out a sigh of joy.

"Niyah," she called shaking out her coat before hanging it on the outside of the closet to dry.

"I'm in the kitchen." In the time since she'd spoken to Betsy, she'd had the opportunity to pull herself together and collect her thoughts. She had no intention of mentioning her conversation with Ms. Betsy to her mother. If Dione could keep secrets, so could she.

Dione hurried into the kitchen, truly happy to see her daughter. "Hey, sweetie," she beamed, and gathered Niyah for a hug. "This is a pleasant surprise, but I would have cooked." She kissed her cheek, then ruffled her short hair.

"I know. But I wanted to do it. Give you a break."

Dione looked around at the pots steaming on the stove, and the dishes set out on the counter. "Seems like you have everything under control. I'm going to get out of these clothes."

"Dinner should be ready in about twenty minutes."

"Sounds good."

Dione went into her bedroom and quickly stripped out of her clothing. As she walked into the bathroom and turned on the shower, she thought about all the questions Niyah was bound to ask and what answers she was going to, or was willing to provide.

She thought she'd successfully explained about the lack of any sign of Christmas at the house, and maybe she would get in the spirit now that Niyah was home. What she was sure her inquisitive daughter would want to hear about was Garrett, a subject that was still too painful to discuss. And if Niyah even remotely thought that she was in some way responsible, she'd badger her until she was given an answer that she believed.

Dione sighed as she stepped under the pulsing water, shutting the shower door behind her. If only the waters would just wash away all the anxiety that rippled through her.

But of course that would be too easy.

Much to her surprise, and relief, all Niyah wanted to talk about was finally getting a break from school, her part-time job in the administrative office, and lo and behold a young man who'd actually captured her daughter's attention.

"So where did you meet Neal?"

"He's in my business management class. He's majoring in economics." She smiled shyly.

"Hmm. Where does he live?" She took a forkful of wild rice.

"He was raised in Maryland, but he's lived in DC for the past ten years."

"Does he live in the dorm or have his own apartment?"

"He has his own place." She paused and looked up at her mother from beneath her long lashes. "I've been there a few times," she said, trying to sound casual. "It's pretty nice. Small."

A wave of anxiety began to take hold. Flashes of her own first love streaked through her mind. She was only a year younger than Niyah when her entire life changed. She didn't want that for her daughter. Niyah had a brilliant, bright future ahead of her and she didn't need it being derailed because of emotions that ran out of control.

"I hope you're not letting Neal interfere with your studies," she said, taking a sip of fruit punch.

Niyah put down her fork and stared across the table at her mother. There was so much she wanted to blurt out — tell her that she understood her worries, her concerns that her life would turn upside down like hers had been. But she didn't. She put the ball in her mother's court.

"Ma. Why don't you just say what's on your mind? You want to know if Neal and I have been intimate. Well, *so far,* the answer is no."

Dione released a shaky breath.

"But if and when I decide that's what I want to do, I know how to protect myself. You taught me well, remember?"

Dione pressed her lips together in a tight smile. "I'm glad to hear that. But sex goes beyond just protection, Niyah. It's a commitment, not just of your body but of your emotions. And if it's not, then it shouldn't be happening in the first place."

Niyah nodded. "I know. That's why I'm waiting."

"Good. I can't ask for more than that. Just be careful," she said softly.

"I will." Niyah put her elbows on the table, thankful that Betsy wasn't in the room to knock them out from under her. "Tomorrow, I'm going to put some Christmas cheer in this place. While you're at work, I'm going shopping. Then I'll meet you at the job and we can pick up a tree."

Dione grinned. "I'm glad you're home."

"So am I."

When Niyah pulled up in a cab in front of Chances Are the following afternoon, she had to get Brenda to come out and help her with her trunkload of packages. She had enough decorations to fill Times Square in Manhattan.

"Girl, what in the world are you going to do with all of this stuff?" Brenda asked, dropping the last of the bags on the office floor.

"We're going to jazz this place up, then I'm taking the rest to my house and do the same thing," she said with a grin. "And I'm recruiting all the help I can get." She pulled off her parka and hung it in the closet. "Any of the girls home?"

"Everyone except Gina. She got her GED results back today and she went out to celebrate."

"She passed!"

"Yep."

"Hallelujah. I know Ma will be happy. Gina's one of her pets."

"We want to wait until the party to tell her."

Niyah's eyes sparkled. "Perfect. It'll fit in with the rest of my plan."

"Which is?" Brenda gave her a suspicious look.

Niyah sat down on the edge of the desk and lowered her voice. "Is my mother around?"

"No," Brenda whispered, caught up in the suspense. "She had to go to a meeting at

Borough Hall. She should be back around four."

"This is what I was thinking, but I need you and Ms. Betsy's help . . ."

When Dione returned to Chances from her meeting, the house was abuzz of activity. Her eyes widened in surprise at the huge wreath with a big red bow that hung from the front door. She looked up at the building and every window had been sprayed with canned snow, and pictures of black Santa Clauses hung from each one. When she stepped inside, gold and green garland was wrapped around the banisters, and mistletoe hung over doorways. Pictures of reindeer pranced along the walls in the corridor.

From the visiting room stereo the sounds of "White Christmas" could be heard as the girls rushed up and down the stairs shouting out for "More tape," and "Anybody got any thumbtacks?" or "That's for my door, you thief."

Dione smiled, infused by a new energy.

"Hi, Ms. Williams," Kisha said, rushing past her. "Ms. Betsy wants all this stuff downstairs," she breathlessly explained as she ran down the stairs, holding a box full of lights and Christmas balls.

Dione grinned. "Be careful running down those stairs, Kisha," she warned, as she sidestepped her and went into the office. A fully decorated, miniature Christmas tree spun slowly on a pedestal atop Brenda's desk.

Brenda was busy stapling up a cutout of a sled on the bulletin board behind her desk.

"Where in the world did all of this stuff come from?"

Brenda turned. "Your daughter. She's been the commander in chief around here today."

Dione smiled and shook her head. "Where is she?"

"Probably downstairs giving out more orders. She said she wanted this place to have some Christmas spirit by any means necessary," she said, chuckling. "Even has Betsy hopping. And you know that takes some doing."

"Let me go see what my child is up to."

Dione went downstairs and stopped short at the door to the child-care room. It resembled a winter wonderland. There was a four-foot plastic blow-up of Santa in his sled and all his reindeer right in the middle of the floor. A Nativity scene sat in the corner illuminated by tiny white lights. Styrofoam snowballs hung from the ceiling, interspersed with rows of silver tinsel.

The toddlers ran around totally enchanted by all the sights, their faces beaming with delight as they squealed and pointed at the decorations.

Niyah was on her knees pulling out gift wrapped packages from shopping bags.

Betsy looked up from unraveling the string of lights as Dione walked fully into the room.

"What can I do to help?" she asked.

Niyah turned and smiled at her mother. "You can start over there," she said pointing to a stack of holiday cutouts to be put up on the walls.

Dione went over to the pile and began taping snowmen, and pictures of gift boxes on the wall, quietly humming "Silent Night," as she worked.

Niyah turned to Betsy and they both smiled.

After an extensive search for just the right tree and a quick meal at McDonald's, Dione and Niyah finally went home. Too exhausted to do more than sit the tree in its stand, Niyah promised that after a good night's sleep she would have their place in shape the following evening. Dione made her promise to wait until she got home.

"I want us to do it together."

"Like always."

"Yes. Like always."

She kissed her mother's cheek. "Good night."

"Good night, sweetheart."

Niyah dragged herself into her room and shut the door. Shortly after she heard her mother's bedroom door close and then the sound of the shower followed.

Niyah thought about what she'd done — the lines she'd crossed. But her mother would just have to forgive her. It was for her own good. Maybe now the ghosts that haunted her mother would be set free. It was time that her mother realized that she was a big girl now and although she understood her mother's reason for wanting to protect her, it was time she realized that it was okay to let go. And maybe when everything was said and done, her mother could finally accept the happiness that she deserved.

But what if it backfired?

Her stomach tensed. It couldn't. It just couldn't.

CHAPTER 19

On the morning of Christmas Eve the aromas of baking, basting, roasting and boiling filled the building, rising up from the kitchen in the basement.

Everyone was up bright and early, including Gina who was determined to cook her first turkey, with Betsy's supervision. Denise had been delegated to supervise the children since everyone knew her cooking skills were suspect. Her smoke alarm still went off religiously at least once per week.

Kisha was in charge of kneading the dough for the half dozen pies they were set to bake and Niyah was more than happy to help with that chore. Even Theresa, who had always been resistant to joining in with any group activity, was busy cutting up cheese for the pans of macaroni.

Brenda was busy pouring seltzer into the fruit punch bowls and supervising some of the other girls who were tossing salads and cutting up the collards. Dione was arranging the last of the gifts beneath the tree, which the whole house had spent half the night before decorating.

Dione looked around, a mixture of joy and melancholy volleying for position. Seeing the girls, hearing their laughter and being witness to the transformation of many of them warmed her. Yet, there was still something missing. For all that she tried to accomplish, she still felt an emptiness. Not so much because there was always more she could do — better, but the need that she longed to be fulfilled in her heart.

Soon, as Betsy said, Niyah would be truly off on her own. Since she'd been home she talked more and more about Neal and she heard the whispered conversations on the phone and the soft laughter. Although Neal may not be "the one" it would be soon.

She looked around watching the children, and their mothers. Soon they all would be gone as well, taking with them whatever she was able to give, only to be replaced by more like them. As long as she was able to keep Chances Are open. And she believed she would.

But where would she be in five, ten years? Who would she come home to at the end of the day?

■ ■ ■ ■

With the cooking all but done and her mother safely upstairs with Brenda and out of the way, Niyah gathered the girls together in the kitchen.

"Now, everybody knows what they're supposed to do, right?" Niyah asked.

A chorus of "yes" and head nodding went around the space.

"She still doesn't know anything does she?" Kisha asked.

"Nope. It's a surprise."

"They putting us on tape again?" Theresa quizzed.

"Yes. This is the last of it," Betsy responded. "So try to be on your best behavior."

A round of grumbles bounced around.

"They should be here soon," Niyah said, and hoped that Garrett would have a change of heart and show up. "So let's start putting the food out on the table and getting the chairs set up."

One by one they began to disperse, leaving Niyah and Betsy alone.

"Did you hear from him?" Betsy asked.

Niyah shook her head.

"Well, if it's meant to be, it will, chile.

Nothing more you can do." She patted Niyah's cheek.

"Looks like we're going to have some kind of feast, Dee. Those girls really did a great job," Brenda said.

"They certainly did." She heard a car pull to a stop out front, and peeked out the window. Her heart knocked. It was the Ford Explorer.

Dione turned away, heat spread through her and her head began to pound. She'd looked forward to and dreaded this day. She hadn't spoken to him in weeks and didn't know how he would react when he saw her again. She knew she'd hurt him, and she needed to let him know how sorry she was about how poorly she'd handled things — that it wasn't his fault. She needed to do that, for herself and for Garrett.

The front doorbell rang. She went to open it, suddenly needing to see him.

Jason walked in, followed by Najashi.

"Hi, Merry Christmas," Dione greeted, stepping aside to let them in. She looked over Najashi's shoulder, thinking Garrett must be pulling up the rear.

"Same to you," Jason said.

"Happy holidays," Najashi said.

"I just need to go and get the rest of the

equipment," Jason said, putting down a camera.

"It's just the two of you?" Dione asked, her heart thundering.

"Yep. Gary said he had things to do today and for us to finish up."

"Mmm. Something sure smells good," Najashi commented, picking up the camera. "Okay if I go down and start setting up?"

"Sure," Dione answered absently. "And of course you're both welcome to join us for dinner."

"Thanks," they chorused.

Dione walked back into the office, forcing a smile onto her face. "They're going to get set up," she said to Brenda.

"I'm going to go down and give Niyah and Betsy a hand with those girls and the kids so we can start serving dinner."

"Okay. I'll be down in a minute."

When Brenda left the room, Dione took a seat at her desk. The Rolodex was open to the Ls. There were Garrett's numbers. She looked at the phone, thought about calling him and what she would say. But she knew if she sat there long enough she'd think of a million reasons why she shouldn't. She started to pick it up just as the doorbell rang.

It was Jason with the rest of the equipment. She got up to answer the door.

Maybe it was best to just leave it alone, she decided as she followed Jason downstairs.

Dinner was everywhere. Literally. Especially all over the faces and hands of the children, who relished in making a supreme mess. All the mothers and the staff pitched in to clean up. And every moment was captured on tape.

"Looks like everyone had a good time," Betsy said dumping empty paper plates in the kitchen garbage bin.

"They sure did," Niyah chuckled. "Those girls can burn."

"Humph. Couldn't say as much when they first got here."

"A lot of them have come a long way."

"Hmm."

"Where's Brenda?"

"I sent her upstairs to keep a look out. Soon as they get here, we can get started."

"Hope it's soon. I'm getting nervous."

Betsy eyed her. "Nervous about what, chile? What you got cooking up your sleeve?"

"You'll see."

"What are you two yapping about?" Dione asked, walking into the kitchen with

301

another stack of paper plates and empty cups.

"Nothing," they said in unison.

Dione looked at them suspiciously. "Well these kids are getting tired. I thought we could open the gifts now."

"That could wait a minute, we have —" She looked over her mother's head to see Brenda giving her a thumbs-up sign.

Dione turned and Brenda plastered an engaging grin on her face.

"What is going on?"

"Why don't you just go up front and relax," Betsy instructed. "We have everything under control."

"That's what I'm afraid of." She walked out, totally undone.

Moments later, Niyah and Betsy walked into the room. Niyah called for everyone's attention.

"If everyone could take a seat, we can get started with the program."

All the girls started giggling and whispering, taking surreptitious glances in Dione's direction, as they took seats around the room.

Program? Something was definitely up, Dione mused, checking the sneaky looking expression on everyone's face.

Betsy walked over to Dione. "Come sit next to me, chile."

"Betsy, what in the world is going on?" she whispered. "What program?"

"Just hush and enjoy. It's something everyone pitched in to do."

Brenda dimmed the lights from the back of the room.

Niyah cleared her throat. "Before we get started, I just want to thank everyone for all their help and cooperation in putting this evening together." She looked in her mother's direction. "Ma, for the past five years you've devoted your time, energy and love to Chances Are and all the young women and their children who have been lucky enough to find refuge here. So, tonight is your night. A chance to say thank you for all that you've done."

Dione began to feel shaky all over. Her heart was racing and a knot caught in her throat. She bit down on her bottom lip as Betsy squeezed her hand, just as Terri tiptoed in and took a seat next to Dione. She kissed her cheek and beamed.

"You were in on this, too?" Dione hissed through her teeth.

"Can't have a this-is-your-life party without me," she teased.

"A few of the girls — current, and from

the past — have some things they want to share," Niyah continued. "Gina, you want to come up?"

Gina took a breath, eased by some of the girls and went up front. She looked out into the audience. "Ms. Dione, when I first got here, I was scared. Scared that I would never be nothing more than a statistic. A seventeen-year-old with a baby and no education. I never had anyone who believed in me, or made me feel that I could ever be more than I was, until I came here and met you." She looked down at her shoes, then out at Dione. "At first all those mornings when you used to sneak up to my room and make sure I got up to go to school, I would get pissed — I mean annoyed," she grinned. "I thought you were just being a pain. But then I started liking my classes and I made friends and started getting good grades again. And even though I gave you and Ms. Betsy a hard time, you never gave up on me." She grinned broadly, her eyes glistening. "Well, I got my GED, Ms. Dione! I got it." She pulled out the treasured piece of paper from her shirt pocket and held it up.

The whole room erupted in applause and rounds of "You go girl!"

Dione stood up as Gina walked away from the front and over to her. Dione embraced her, holding her tight, feeling Gina's tiny body shake with her tears. "Congratulations," she whispered against her veil of braids, sniffing back her own tears. "I knew you could do it."

"Thank you, Ms. Dione," she mumbled. "For everything." She stepped back and took her seat as Niyah came back up front.

"Ma, I used to watch you come home at night, sometimes elated because of some success of one of the girls or when one of the babies took their first step, and sometimes I would see the sadness in your eyes when you thought you'd tried as hard as you could to reach one of them and believed that you hadn't. Most of you don't know these two young ladies. They were here when the house first opened and they gave my mother and the whole staff a rough time. But I think they have something they want to say. Lynn and Pauline."

Everyone turned when the two well-dressed young women came through the door and walked up front.

"Oh my God," Dione whispered to Betsy. "Lynn and Pauline. I don't believe it. I haven't heard from them since they left."

Betsy patted her hand.

Dione had worried long and hard about Pauline and Lynn. They were two of the most difficult residents she'd ever dealt with. All of her training and education had not prepared her for their anger and resentment toward everyone and everything that tried to come near them. Both of them had been abused. Lynn by her stepfather, Pauline by her drug-addicted mother. They'd both spent the better part of their youth moving from one group home or foster-care setting to another, until they were finally referred to Chances by a social worker who'd heard of the privately-run facility.

After the first month of their arrival, Dione had begun to have serious doubts about the effectiveness of Chances and that maybe she couldn't have made a difference. But it seemed as though the more those two resisted her help, the more determined she became to succeed.

Looking at them now, listening to their success, she knew her efforts and her faith had not been in vain.

"I don't know how many times Ms. Dione needed to put us out and didn't," Lynn was saying, her nut-brown face having softened from the hard lines it once held since she'd left nearly four years earlier. "We tried to do everything we could to break every rule of the house, from staying out overnight, to cussing the staff out. But she never gave up on us." Lynn turned to Pauline.

"Every day she made sure we got up to go to school. Checked on us when our kids were sick. She even helped me study for a test after I told her just what she could do with her stupid housing preparation class," Pauline admitted with a crooked smile. "I'd been kicked out of so many places by the time I'd gotten to Chances Are, I just figured it would only be a matter of time before I got thrown out of here, too. But it never happened. And I never got the chance to say thank you for that, Ms. Dione. Thank you. I'm working now at a law firm, of all places," she said laughing. "And —" She held up her left hand. "I'm engaged."

Everyone started clapping and oohing and ahhing at Pauline's ring.

"I just want you to know, Ms. Dione," Lynn picked up when the noise died down. "I have a fulltime job as an administrative assistant at the Legal Aid Society and I'm in my second year of college at Hunter studying for my social work degree. And I know I couldn't have done it without you pushing me to believe that I was better than I'd been told I was. Thank you from the bottom of my heart."

They both walked over to Dione amidst

clapping and stomping and showered her with hugs and kisses.

"This is incredible," she choked to Betsy, wiping her eyes.

"You deserve it, chile. Everybody needs to know that they're cared about and appreciated."

Garrett stood in the shadows of the back of the room, overcome by the love and adoration being showered on Dione. Deep inside he knew that above all she was a wonderful person, but a full understanding of the impact she had on people's lives hadn't hit him until then.

One after another the girls came up to express to Dione how important she was to them, how she had made them feel human again and worthwhile. Denise surprised everyone when she told them she'd gotten her apartment and would be able to move out at the end of the year. "Don't forget your smoke detector," Kisha shouted out.

Even Theresa stood up to tell them how important being there had been for her and that even though she gave them all a hard time when she first arrived, Dione never gave up and kept pushing her and talking to her even when she wouldn't talk back.

Niyah stepped back up to the front. She

clasped her hands in front of her. "This evening has been a tribute to my mother, an opportunity to say thank you for what she's done, how she's influenced your lives. But the one story that hasn't been told is mine. All my life I knew, believed that my mother loved me unconditionally. But it wasn't until recently that I truly understood how much.

"Many of you may think that my mother is just a real nice lady with a good education who wants to do the right thing. My mother is much more than that. She's more like all of you than you know."

Dione's body stiffened. Betsy clasped her hand a bit tighter.

"When my mother was seventeen . . ." she began.

As Garrett listened to Niyah unveil the young life of Dione, his emotions seesawed from one extreme to the other: outrage at what her parents had done, agony for what she'd gone through and total awe and admiration for the woman she'd become, anyway. And through it all, she loved her daughter so much that she was willing to risk everything to protect her. Everything, including her own happiness.

There was no question in his mind that

this was so much more than just a good feeling inside. It was about sacrifice, about giving a part of yourself for someone else completely. And maybe, just maybe, his own mother, in her own twisted, inexperienced way gave him up because she loved him enough to know that she could never take care of him and maybe someone else could.

Love was about taking risks with your emotions and not backing down from what was in your heart. He'd never been willing to take the risk with his feelings, to put them on the line. All those years he'd held back, blaming everyone, never giving them the chance to care. Dione didn't back away because she didn't care about him. She backed away because she did.

Dione covered her face with her hands as her tears rolled unchecked down her face, slowly shaking her head. All these years she could have shared her private burden with her daughter, with these girls who were reaching out to her to help her carry it.

Niyah understood. She didn't hate her for the lies she'd told. She understood that it was because she loved her that she'd hidden the truth. She turned to Betsy who clasped her around the shoulder, pulling her closer like she used to do when she was a teenager living in her house.

"I want to thank you, Ma, for everything. For the sacrifices you made for me. For the meals you didn't eat so that I could. For the hours you spent working to keep a roof over our heads when you needed to study so you could get out of school, for making me believe that I was special," she said her voice shaking with emotion. "And most of all thank you for loving me so hard and so much." Her eyes filled. "I love you, Ma, for everything," she said walking across the room. "All that stuff, it doesn't matter. You and Ms. Betsy are all the family I need." She walked into her mother's arms and everyone in the room stood and applauded between their tears.

"I love you, Ma," she whispered over and again. "You gave me a chance to be everything I can be. Now it's your turn."

Garrett wanted to go to her, tell her how he felt, tell her how incredible she was and how much he understood why she felt compelled to end things with him. But he didn't want to intrude on the private moment between her and Niyah.

This was her night.

All the girls and their children clamored around showering her with kisses and hugs. He turned to leave, but not before Dione caught a glimpse of him walking out the door.

CHAPTER 20

Niyah was up before the sun, eager as always to dig under the tree and hunt out her gifts. And as usual she made it a point of hopping down on her mother's bed to wake her up.

"Merry Christmas, Ma." She bounced on the bed. "Wake up, it's Christmas."

Dione slowly pulled the comforter away from her face and looked bleary eyed at Niyah who appeared as bright and alert as if she'd been up for hours.

"It can't be Christmas already," Dione groaned. "I just went to bed a few minutes ago." Her head swam with thoughts and images of the night before. The words of love and praise. The glorious feeling that she really had done the right things, and the sight of Garrett walking out of the door without saying a word. She stretched. "You're going to wake up Betsy," she warned, hoping that would fend Niyah off for a moment.

"Too late. She's already up fixing break-fast."

"Breakfast," she groaned again. "How can anyone even think of eating after all the food we consumed last night?" Dione pulled the cover back over her face.

Niyah shook her. "Come on. Get up." She hopped up off the bed. "If I don't see you out there in five minutes I'm coming back," she warned, and Dione knew she meant it.

Dione turned over on her side in the vain hope of catching just a few more minutes of sleep. But the excited voice of Niyah, squealing over her gifts just like she always did, dashed that hope. Dione pulled herself out of bed, ducked in the bathroom for a quick wash up then joined Niyah and Betsy in the living room.

Before she knew it, she was wrapped up in the merriment as they sat among the shredded mounds of gift wrap, colored ribbons, bows and empty boxes.

Betsy was thrilled with her robe and modeled it proudly. Niyah had given her a watch, which she insisted she wear and stop telling the time by the angle of the sun.

Dione immediately put on the gold locket that Niyah had given her with the tiny picture of Niyah at her high school graduation inside.

Niyah put the sterling silver pen and pencil set that Betsy had gotten for her inside the Kenneth Cole bag from her mother, then sauntered off to her room, bouncing to some unknown beat coming from the CD player from Terri.

Dione sat back and took a breath. Momentarily closing her eyes.

"That was some night, last night," Betsy said.

"That it was," Dione sighed.

"I have a gift for you, too," Betsy said. "Wait right here." She went into the bedroom and came out several moments later and handed Dione an envelope.

Dione looked at it in confusion. "What is this?"

"It's a letter. From your mother. Seems like she saw that PSA on television and decided to write. It came to Chances a few days ago. The envelope that one came in," she said, pointing to the envelope in Dione's hand, "was addressed to me. She wanted me to make sure you got it, *if* I thought it would be all right." She smiled softly. "I think it is." She turned away and walked out of the room.

Dione stared down at the white envelope and her hand began to shake. A gamut of emotions ran through her at once: hate, fright, betrayal, longing and love. Emotions she hadn't wanted to admit she could still feel for her parents. But they were still there, clinging beneath the surface needing to be nurtured.

She took a shaky breath and slowly ripped the envelope open.

My dearest Dione,

I know you must still hate me for what I allowed to happen to you so many years ago. There hasn't been a day that you haven't been on my mind and in my heart. I live with my guilt and my weakness every day of my life. I want you to know that I never stopped loving you even though you must believe that I did. You were and still are the most precious thing in the world to me.

Back then, I was weak. I was fearful of your father's wrath and whether you believe it or not, I sent you away to protect you. I couldn't bear the thought of him hurting you like that again. But I should have been stronger. I should have stood up to him and I didn't. I know that all the apologies in the world could never make up for what you must have gone through. But I am sorry, Dione.

Your father was never the same after that night. His anger and his disappointment just kept eating away at him day by day. He had wanted so much for his baby girl and all he could see was that all his hopes for you were gone.

We moved away shortly after that night to Washington. It was as if he wanted to put everything behind him. But he couldn't. He died last year. But the last thing he said to me before he passed was to try to find you and tell you he was sorry and how much he'd always loved you. Your father was a hard man, but inside he was a good man, Dione. I hope you can believe that and forgive him.

When I saw your face on television and listened to what it was you were doing, I knew my prayers had been answered. You were alive and safe and doing, it seems, what you were called to do.

I know you probably don't want to see me, or have anything to do with me, and if so, I'll find a way to understand. But I hope you can find it in your heart to forgive me and hopefully give me a chance to see my grandchild. I have enclosed my address in the hope that you will come to see me. I would welcome you and my grandchild with open arms.

Always,
Your loving mother

Dione held the letter to her breast almost as if she wanted to squeeze the words out, make them a part of her. How many nights had she lain awake praying, shedding silent tears for the loss of her parents' love? They had never stopped loving her. They loved her in the only way they knew how.

"Oh, Mama," she wept, as the tears of exoneration finally flowed from her eyes. She was worthy of love and always had been.

Dione stopped brushing her hair in mid-stroke at the light tap on her bedroom door.

"Come in," she said thickly.

Betsy stepped into the room. "You all right, Dee?"

Dione turned around and smiled. "Yes. Finally Betsy. Finally." She crossed the room and gathered Betsy in her arms. "Thank you Betsy for saving me from myself so many times. For taking us in and giving me what I needed all these years even when I didn't want it. For being a mother to me and a grandmother to my child. She always loved me, Betsy. Always. My daddy, too."

"Hard to stop loving a child," she clucked, patting Dione on the back. "If anyone knows that it's you." She stepped back and looked Dione up and down. "And where are you off to?"

Dione adjusted her beige cable knit sweater over her hips. "I have some unfinished business to take care of." She sniffed over a wobbly grin. Her hazel eyes sparkled.

"It's about time." Betsy shook her head and slowly walked out. "Sure enough."

When Dione stepped out into the early Christmas morning, everywhere that she looked was covered in a thin blanket of snow. It fell from the heavens in fat puffs, frolicking on rooftops, and doing little jigs along the streets before settling. She held her face up letting the wetness caress her, inhaling the pureness of the air as the snow bathed everything in its path in newness.

She was filled with euphoria as she skipped over to her car and began brushing the snow from the windshield. Let him be home, she silently chanted. As she worked the sound of music broke through the stillness. She straightened as Johnny Mathis's voice became clearer. "Chances are, though

I wear a silly grin the moment you come into view . . ."

Her heart beat a bit faster as a car came to a stop next to hers.

Garrett stepped out of the car and the music surrounded them. "Anyone can see, you're the only one for me . . ."

"Hi," he said from the far side of the car.

A slow smile broke out across her face. "Hi."

"Going somewhere?"

"As a matter of fact, I was coming to see you."

He came around to stand in front of her. His eyes ran over her face. "I was a fool to almost let you get away, Dee."

"No more than me for sending you." She stepped off the curb and right up to him.

He reached out and stroked her cheek, brushing away a snowflake. "You were right, Chances Are is a magical place. It's a place for growth and change. I know it happened to me, but it's because of the energy that you bring to it, Dione. I wanted to fight what was happening. I didn't want to give in. I wanted to hang on to my pain and anger, my resentment. But," he slowly shook his head, "there comes a time in life when you finally have to let go, Dee. No one can be held responsible for our happiness, or who we are and become, but us."

His eyes skipped across the planes of her face, memorizing each dip, the soft lines, the slope of her eyes, the fullness of her lips.

"Listening to Niyah last night, brought everything together for me. I was so stuck on me being the only one who'd ever been hurt, it blinded me to the world around me. Understanding your struggle and how you used your adversity to draw strength, gave me the strength I needed to finally make peace within myself. To let go, move forward."

Tears trickled from her eyes onto his hand. Gently he brushed them from her cheeks.

"I was foolish not to let you get close, to keep a part of me away from you," Dione said in a tight voice. "But I've held on to the belief that I didn't deserve to be truly happy for so long, I just didn't know any other way. What happened to me at seventeen colored my entire life and what I thought about myself." She clasped his hand that caressed her face. "I believed that protecting Niyah from my own ugly truth, my own lack of feeling worthy, was my way of loving her.

"Maybe it was. But I never gave her a chance to decide for herself. And that was wrong. Love is a lot of crazy mixed up things, give and take. It will make you go to extreme lengths for those you love. But love is also about honesty. I know that now, and in discovering it, I nearly lost you in the process."

His thumb brushed across her bottom lip and she felt her insides begin to heat. "This is the first Christmas in my life that I've ever wanted to celebrate, Dee. I want to keep the magic going from this Christmas on."

"What are you saying?"

"I'm saying, chances are I'm crazy in love with you and I'm not taking any chances on losing you ever again. Is that honest enough for you?"

She draped her hands around his neck. "Merry Christmas, Garrett Lawrence. I love you."

"Merry Christmas, Dee." He lowered his head and kissed her for all the world to see, his spirit seeming to soar and float free like the flakes that danced around them. "Let's celebrate this wonderful holiday at my place," he whispered against her mouth. "I'll even let you drive."

She looked into his eyes for a long, hot moment. "I do believe some major celebrating is in order."

Laughing, they walked arm in arm to Garrett's car. Dione stopped just before getting in. "I'd like you to come with me and Niyah to Washington," she said, smiling. "There's someone there I haven't seen in a very long time. And I'll even let you drive."

"On one condition," he teased.

"What's that?"

"On the way, would you promise to tell me how you know Nick Ashford and Valerie Simpson?" he said in a little boy voice.

Dione tossed her head back and laughed, the tinkle of it floating along the stillness of the winter-white morning.

"Maybe you can convince me when we get to your house."

"Baby, the pleasure will be mine."

Niyah looked down on them from the window and smiled. "Merry Christmas, you guys," she whispered.

As Dione lay cuddled in Garrett's arms, snug beneath the down comforter, his slow, steady breathing a soothing anchor for her soul, she felt true joy. This was happiness, this weightless euphoria that had eluded her.

This Christmas Day was one she'd never forget. She'd maintained the love and respect of her daughter, she'd rediscovered the love she'd thought she'd lost with her parents and she'd finally found the spark, the fire that had been missing in her life, by giving herself the chance to love Garrett from the depths of her soul and let him love her back.

She was sure they'd have a rocky road ahead of them. Both of them were stubborn, determined and driven to succeed. And they both had their issues that would still take time to heal, but the healing process had begun. And she knew the one thing they had that would sustain them was their strength of spirit. The hard-fought battle of their pasts was won. They'd bared their souls, withstood the vision and had still chosen each other.

She sighed, a soft smile framing her face as she adjusted her body closer to the contours of Garrett's. Chances Are *was* a magical place. Truly, she believed it now.

EPILOGUE

Six months later

Chances Are received two major grants, one from the Fordham Foundation and another from the Holt Foundation as a result of the documentary that aired across the country on major cable stations. More funding was on the way and organizations around the nation were asking for Dione's help in establishing facilities similar to Chances Are.

After that first visit to Washington at the beginning of the New Year, Dione and her mother began the painful process of trying to restore the lost years. Dione made it a point to call her mother at least twice a week, and Niyah visited her grandmother regularly on the weekends, she even brought Neal over to visit. And whenever Niyah had a break from her classes at Howard, she stopped by to run errands or just to sit and talk. Funny, they were so close for so long and never knew it. Yet, for both Dione and

Niyah, Betsy would always have a special place in their hearts.

Gina was able to get her first "real" job as a result of getting her GED, and would soon be ready to move into her own apartment. Theresa's special reading classes were so successful, she'd become interested in becoming a reading therapist. Denise no longer set off the smoke detector in her new apartment thanks to Ms. Betsy who insisted on standing over her while she cooked to check the flame, in the last week before she moved out. Denise finally got the hang of it.

And soon they would be replaced by others and the process of love and rebuilding would begin again.

Dione Williams-Lawrence tours the country now, openly telling her story and speaking to schools, women's organizations and community groups about teen pregnancy — the good and the bad — and the need for the reform of group homes and the foster-care system, and most importantly education on prevention. And on all of her trips, and during those long days and late nights, her greatest fan is her husband, her friend, her confidant — Garrett.